A MORE THAN MAYHEM
Christmas

A MORE THAN MAYHEM
Christmas

JAY McLEAN

AUTHOR NOTE

A More Than Mayhem Christmas is a 35k word novella, and the sixth book in the More Than Series. To avoid spoilers and get to know the characters, it's best to read the previous books in the series first.

To Sam Shemeld
A Logan Matthews Girl From Day One

GUEST LIST

JAKE
MLB PRO

MIKAYLA
MLB WAG

LOGAN
RESIDENT DOCTOR

AMANDA
CHILD PSYCHOLOGIST

CAMERON
ARCHITECT

LUCY
BOOKSTORE OWNER

DYLAN
MAYHEM MOTORS

RILEY
DYLAN'S BOSS

SPECIAL APPEARANCE

HEIDI
RETAIL BUYER

1

Cameron

"Grandpa, push!" my daughter, Katie, squeals, her hands out in front of her, reaching for Mark from a good twenty feet away. She's strapped into a swing attached to a two-story rocket ship with a slide coming out of the top floor. The new play set was her Christmas gift from my parents, and I stand in the middle of their backyard, my arms crossed, glare in place.

"You never got *me* anything this cool," I murmur.

Next to me, Mark, my *dad who stepped up*, chuckles under his breath. "One, you're almost thirty. Get over it. And two, you were *six* when I met you."

I shrug. "Still..."

"And besides, I bought you a *Delorean*."

A massive grin immediately replaces my fake scowl, and I drop my arms to my sides, stand taller, prouder. "So, what you're saying is, I'm *still* your favorite?"

"Grandpa!" Katie squeals again.

Mark jogs toward her, saying, "Coming, sweetheart!"

"Wait!" I call out. "You didn't answer my question!"

I watch as he replaces my mom behind Katie and catches her at the highest point, whispering something in her ear that makes her giggle, before pushing her forward.

"I'll always be his favorite, right?" I mumble, slowly trailing my gaze from the play set to my wife waiting beside me, the disapproval in her eyes unmistakable. "What?" I ask.

"You're competing with your two-year-old daughter."

I sigh. Then smirk. "I'm *your* favorite, right?

Lucy giggles, breaking her facade, and steps closer to me. "You're my favorite... *idiot.*"

I throw my hands in the air, basking in the victory, before hugging her close. "I'll take it."

Mom approaches, rolling her eyes as she takes Lucy from my arms and straight into hers. "Are you being needy again?" she asks me, then pulls back slightly to look Luce in the eyes. "How are you feeling, sweetheart?"

"Tired," Luce says through a sigh, and whatever Mom sees in her expression has her taking Lucy's hand and leading her away.

My heart falters a beat, and I begin to follow them. Mom must sense my movements, because she turns to me, her arm going around Lucy's shoulders as she shakes her head at me. I stop in my tracks and then reluctantly nod.

I know this is their time, and I need to let them have it, but that doesn't mean I don't hurt for my wife and, admittedly, for me.

Holidays have become harder for Lucy ever since we became parents. Not only does she miss her mom, but she wants so badly to be the type of mother she was blessed with, that her mind's constantly plagued with fears of falling short.

Just to be clear, I couldn't have dreamed of a better mother for our daughter.

Unfortunately, no amount of affirmation coming from me can seem to change her mind.

That's when my mom steps in.

They had always gotten along, and there's no doubt my mom loves Lucy as if she were her own, but once Lucy became pregnant, their bond became greater, and then even more so once Katie was born.

I think it elevated one night when Katie was just a few weeks old. I was exhausted, but Luce—she'd barely closed her eyes since the moment she knew she was going into labor. Lucy had experience with newborns since she was around to help her mom with all six of her younger brothers, but the only aspect of parenting she was new to was breastfeeding... and it was the only thing she seemed to struggle with. It was close to 3 a.m. one night when we were both sitting up in bed, my daughter in my wife's arms, as Katie cried out loud and Lucy cried in silence. Tears streamed down Luce's cheeks, and I watched them both, helpless, not knowing who to comfort more. Katie wasn't latching on like she should and, of course, Lucy blamed herself. "I don't know what I'm doing wrong," she'd sobbed, over and over, and it had been the same the past three times Katie had woken crying and hungry.

It affected Luce mentally as much as it did physically, and I didn't know how to fix it. Honestly, I wanted to cry for the both of them. But then Lucy looked up at me, her eyes filled with liquid heartache, and said the words I'd been keeping to myself. "I think I need your mom."

The phone barely rang before Mom answered, as if she'd been expecting it. She was at our cabin within minutes and in our room within seconds. She handed me Katie and asked for a moment alone with Lucy. For minutes that felt like hours, I attempted to soothe a crying Katie in my arms while I paced the living room. My chest ached every time my daughter opened her eyes—blue, just like her mother's, like her grandmother's—a woman I'd never met, but who I spoke to that night. I asked her to help her daughter—my *wife*—because she was drowning under the weight of her own expectations, and I could feel her struggle to stay afloat.

After what felt like forever, Mom called me back into the bedroom, where Lucy was in bed, on her side, her eyes clear of tears for the first time in hours. I looked at my mom, who offered a reassuring smile, and then I listened to her advice as she showed me how to place Katie so she could feed while Lucy was lying down. It took a bit of maneuvering to get my two girls *just right*, and then it all just... clicked. Mom stood at the end of the bed, looking down at us—me lying opposite my wife, our daughter between us. I reached across, stroking my wife's cheek as her eyes got heavier and heavier, losing the fight to fake it. Within minutes, she was asleep, and Katie followed soon after.

Mom took Katie into her arms, kissed my cheek, and promised me that things would get better. Easier. And they did.

To this day, I have no idea what was said in that bedroom while I was gone, and I'll never ask. But whatever it was, it changed their relationship forever.

"Are you still pouting about the favorite child thing?" Mark asks now, a smiling Katie sitting on his shoulders. Hands out, finger stretched, she reaches for me just as a yawn escapes me. I take her from him, then attack her cheek and neck, pretending to bite her. She squirms in my arms and giggles loudly—the greatest sound in the entire world, but I'm biased, obviously.

"Daddy silly, isn't he?" Mark asks her.

"Silly Daddy," she repeats, kicking out her legs—a sign for me to put her back down. The second her feet touch the grass, she's off again, running around my parents' backyard, kicking up fallen leaves with her tiny little boots.

"She has so much energy," Mark chuckles, standing beside me while Katie runs toward a giant oak tree.

"I know. I don't know where she gets it," I reply, my words muffled by another yawn.

Katie had woken us up just before five this morning, jumping on the bed and yelling, "Mama! Daddy! Santa came! Santa came!"

Luce and I had just gotten to sleep a few hours earlier after spending the night wrapping the insane number of gifts we'd gotten her. We had a low-key breakfast, just the three of us, then headed to Lucy's family home for lunch, and then we came here for dinner and to drop Katie off before the mayhem truly begins. It's been a long-ass day, and I'm exhausted. I don't know how Katie is still upright. "Twenty-eleventy-three," Katie shouts from behind the oak tree. "Ready or not, here I come!"

"Shit, were we supposed to be hiding?" Mark mumbles, taking off before I have time to respond. He hides behind a large potted plant, and I climb onto the trampoline and lie flat. If I'm lucky, I might be able to close my eyes for a few minutes.

"Daddy! Grandpa!" Katie shouts. "Where are you?"

"I want to play!" Lucy calls out, and I lift my head to see her and Mom walking toward Katie.

"Let's count again," Mom says, taking Katie's hand and leading her back toward the oak tree. "Give your mama time to hide."

Katie goes willingly, and I wait until Lucy's close before sitting up to help her climb onto the trampoline with me. We lie on our sides, facing each other, the sound of Katie counting made-up numbers filling our ears. "You good?" I ask, hand on her waist as I pull her close.

Lucy nods, her lips curving into a smile. "Do you realize how lucky we are?"

"I know how lucky *I* am. I have you. You, though—you're stuck with me."

Shaking her head, she moves in closer, her lips meeting

mine for all of a millisecond. "I wouldn't want to do life without you."

"Really?" I ask, raising my eyebrows. "Two nights ago, you threatened to murder me in my sleep."

She rolls her eyes, her smile getting wider. "I threaten that every night, and you're still breathing, so..."

"True." I chuckle, bringing her closer so her head's to my chest. "So what you're saying is that you love me, and I'm your favorite."

"You've always been my favorite, and you always will be."

I sigh. "That's all I need to hear."

"Found you, Grandpa!" Katie squeals, and Luce and I separate, lifting our heads to watch them.

"You're so smart! How did you know where I was?" Mark says, poking her sides until she runs away from him. He chases after her, hands out, fingers ready to tickle her some more.

"I think she might be the luckiest girl in the world," I murmur, facing Lucy again. "She has two amazing grandpas."

"And the best grandma," she says.

"*Grandmas*," I correct. "One here, and one watching over her twenty-four-seven."

Lucy smiles at that.

"And enough aunts and uncles to always have her back."

"And the most amazing dad to always protect her," Lucy adds, kissing me once. Then returning for more, deepening the kiss just enough to stir up a lick of fire inside me.

"And the most beautiful, most giving..." I grab her ass, squeeze tight. "Most *sexiest* mom in the entire world."

Luce pulls away and sits up straight, her cheeks flushed. "We're leaving now!" she yells.

I laugh under my breath and hop off the trampoline before helping her down. Mom takes Katie's hand and leads her toward us, saying, "So, you have plans with your friends tonight?"

"Yep," Lucy replies.

"It's so nice that you can all be together for the holidays. I miss them."

Living in a small town, she sees our friends often. It's only Heidi, Jake and Mikayla who moved away, and out of North Carolina. My mom didn't really get to know Heidi well back when we were in high school, and she moved away after college, so she's not around much.

Micky and Jake live in St. Louis now, but Micky's been spending more time here lately, so what my mom is really saying is she misses *Jake*. My mom *loves* Jake. Scratch that. *All* moms love Jake. It's hard not to.

"So, what's the plan?" Mark asks. "You're just going to hang out in your cabin?"

Lucy fake sniffles. "It's the farewell tour, Marky Mark."

Mark hugs her to his side. "I bet y'all have a ton of memories there, huh?"

Lucy pouts for real this time, nodding as she says, "We've been there for so long. It's where we grew up, grew *together*, and where we brought Katie home."

"But you have a beautiful new home where you can make fresh memories," Mom tries to assure. "And how many women get to say they live in a house their husband designed and their brothers built?"

"That's true," Lucy says, moving from Mark's side to mine. She smiles up at me, and I return the expression. Our new house, still built on the Preston property, has been my favorite project to work on because it's *ours*. Luce and I worked tirelessly to make everything perfect in our forever home, and personally, I can't wait to move in there. But Luce—she's a romantic, not just with love but with the memories the cabin holds. We'd practically lived there together since her dad built it for her when we were still in high school. There are a lot of moments tied to the place and a hell of a lot of *firsts*.

"So, what happens to the cabin now?" Mark asks.

"The twins have already claimed it," I answer. Lucy's brothers—Lincoln and Liam—are social media influencers, and so they're turning it into a studio/office.

"Well, have fun tonight," Mom says. "And don't feel you have to rush to pick her up tomorrow."

"She can stay as long as you need," Mark agrees.

"You know we love having her," Mom adds. "And I have no plans for days, just in case you two wanted to get things done while you're off work."

Since I can remember, Mark had always wanted to "take care" of Mom and me, and to him, that meant setting me up for life and giving Mom the option to never have to work again. It took a lot of convincing on his end, but once Katie was born, Mom finally conceded. She has Katie a few days a week while Lucy and I work. *Not* surprisingly, those are also the days Mark seems to have very little going on at his car dealership, so he only works half-days.

On the days Mom doesn't have her, Katie goes to work with Lucy at the bookstore, or she's with Tom, Lucy's dad, or any of her brothers and their girls. Sometimes, it almost becomes a competition to be the one to take care of her. Like I said, Katie's the luckiest girl in the entire world.

"I'll call you tomorrow and let you know how we're holding up," I tell them.

Lucy squats down, hugging our daughter tight. "Be good for Grandma and Grandpa, okay?"

Katie holds her mother's face in her hands, kissing the tip of her nose like she's watched me do a thousand times before. "I be good," she says, then whispers something in Lucy's ear before pulling back.

Lucy sighs. "Just one time. And do it now so it's out of your system."

Katie's eyes go wide with excitement, before looking up at

me, then at her grandparents. She takes a step back, so she's the center of our universe. Then she smirks—crooked, just like her mother's. "One time?" she confirms with Lucy.

"Just once," Luce agrees.

Katie giggles. And then... "Fucking shit."

GUEST LIST

JAKE
MLB PRO

MIKAYLA
MLB WAG

LOGAN
RESIDENT DOCTOR

AMANDA
CHILD PSYCHOLOGIST

CAMERON
ARCHITECT

LUCY
BOOKSTORE OWNER

DYLAN
MAYHEM MOTORS

RILEY
DYLAN'S BOSS

SPECIAL APPEARANCE

HEIDI
RETAIL BUYER

2

Jake

I never realized how much of the world is made up of *threes* until I stopped to really think about it.

In high school, I once did a paper on the rule of threes as it pertained to literature. It's pretty much the only thing I remember learning from high school.

To me, school was a stepping-stone to college, which was another stepping-stone to pro baseball. It's strange to think how high-school-me has everything he ever dreamed of, and yet...

I shove the diamond ring in my pocket before glancing at the bathroom mirror, then the door. On the other side of that door is silence. No footsteps. No movement. Unless Kayla suddenly took off without a word, I know she's there. At least physically. Mentally, I don't know where she is...

The *rule* of three is a literary device used by writers to give their storytelling more impact. Three adjectives, three characters, three acts. Or three simple words.

You can see it in everyday life used by brands as their

slogans. Nike: Just do it; Redbull: gives you wings; Skittles: Taste the rainbow.

Not surprisingly for me, I've always linked the number three to baseball.

Three strikes, and you're *out.*

I glance at my reflection once more. So much has changed in the ten years Kayla and I have been together. We've both grown, that's for sure. In multiple ways. For multiple reasons. And the truth is... I don't know if we've grown closer or further apart.

I tap at the engagement ring in my pocket, making sure it hasn't disappeared into thin air. Then I ignore the shakiness of my hands, the fear in my mind, and the uncertainty turning my stomach before exiting the room.

Kayla's exactly where I left her. In our bed. On her side. Her eyes closed.

We're in the garage apartment of my parents' house, where we moved her into after the tragedy that took her entire family.

I squat down beside the bed and move the hair away from her face so I can see her more clearly. Her eyes open slowly, the brown of her irises meeting mine. One second. Two. *Three.* Then they close again.

"We don't have to go tonight," I tell her, my voice just above a whisper. "I'll call Cam—"

"And tell him what?" she interrupts, her eyes snapping open as she practically throws the covers off her. I watch as she moves to the dresser, pulling open the drawers with enough force it rattles the items atop it.

"I'll just tell him I'm tired," I say, coming to a stand. "He won't—"

"You need to stop making excuses for me, Jake. I'm *fine,*" she says.

Only she's not *fine.*

And she hasn't been for a while.

I don't know what happened or exactly where things went wrong, but she hasn't been herself in quite some time. Maybe I noticed it too late, or maybe she worked really fucking hard to hide it from me. Either way, *fine* is the absolute last word I'd use to describe her.

And *us.*

I bite back a sigh, and instead, use what energy I have left to plead, "Kayla..."

She stops with her task, her shoulders dropping, along with her head. Then she turns to me. Her eyes are clear. No tears. And I wait with bated breath as she approaches me. "I'm sorry," she whispers, right before she wraps her arms around my waist. Face pressed against my chest, she mumbles, "I don't know what's wrong with me."

"There's nothing wrong with you," I assure. A lie, obviously, because this simple hug is the closest we've been that *she's* instigated since I can remember.

Kayla pulls away, and I almost die at the emptiness her touch leaves behind. But then she takes my hand, leads me to the large armchair in the corner of the room. She urges me to sit, and I do as she asks. Then she sits across my lap, her arms going around my neck as she rests her head on my shoulder. "I'm sorry," she repeats.

"Baby..." I stroke her leg, resting the back of my head on the chair, and stare up at the ceiling. I give myself a moment, allowing my lungs to fill with air for the first time in what feels like forever. I don't want to tell her it's okay, because one: I don't truly know what she's apologizing for; and two: I don't want to lie to her. Things aren't okay. *She's* not okay. "You know you can talk to me if something's upsetting you."

She seems to hesitate a moment before answering, "I know."

"Do you?" I ask, needing confirmation.

She pulls away, and I reach for her face, cup her jaw. "I think it's just... being separated so much is getting to me."

Postseason ended early November, but I have training camps and other things that keep me in St. Louis for the most part. I come back here as much as possible, only because *here* is where she chooses to be. I open my mouth, ready to retort, but she beats me to it.

"Please don't take that as anything other than what it is. I'm so proud of you. You *know* I am."

I nod, because it's the one thing I feel sure of. Kayla has been by my side through all my ups and downs. From my college days to the draft, to the injuries, to the trades, and moving to three different states before finally finding my place in St. Louis. That was two years ago and a little later than I wanted for my career, but it is what it is.

Kayla had always found her footing, so to speak, getting to know my teammates and their partners and doing her best to make sure the transition was as easy for me as possible. Because of her, the only thing I've had to worry about is baseball. But... St. Louis has been different. She doesn't go to every home game like she used to, and the ones she does attend, she doesn't sit with the rest of the wives and girlfriends in a suite. Instead, she chooses to sit alone with the rest of the spectators. She attends only the official social events with me, but picks and chooses anything else. The worst part is that for the past few months, I've come home to an empty house half the time. We've lived together since we were eighteen. To say that it's an adjustment is an understatement. The only reason she's given me is that "it doesn't feel like *home*."

I've told her to find a different house.

She said that the house doesn't make a home.

So, instead, she flies here a few times a month and stays in the garage apartment. My parents say that they have an open invite to dinner when she's here, but she declines. They don't see her often, not even coming or going. Our friends tell me the same. She holes up in the apartment, alone, and no one can seem to crack the wall she builds around herself whenever she's here.

I don't know how to fix it, and even if I did, I don't even know what's broken.

"I'm going to get in the shower," she says, breaking through my thoughts. She's up and walking away before I even fully comprehend what she's said.

I wait a few minutes after hearing the shower switch on to go into the bathroom and lean against the counter, my arms crossed, head bowed. I don't say a word, and even though I know she sees me, she doesn't speak either. Not until she's out of the shower with a towel wrapped around her. "God, I feel so much better."

I peer up at her, my eyebrows raised. "Yeah?"

Nodding, she steps up to me, replying, "I think that's exactly what I needed." She kisses me once, twice, and I find myself smiling, even if it's wrong. "I'm so sorry," she adds, and I hold her to me, too afraid to let her go.

"Don't be sorry."

She shakes her head. "And I should apologize to your parents, too. I hope I didn't ruin their Christmas with my shitty mood."

"You didn't," I assure. "You know they love you, right?"

"I know. And I love them, too. So much. Which only makes things a thousand times worse..."

I hold her closer. Tighter. "Is there anything I can do?"

Her body falls into mine, as if every muscle unfurled instantaneously. "Trust me. You're doing it."

"Yeah?"

Her head tilts back, her eyes meeting mine. "You have no idea how much."

I lower my mouth to hers, basking in the way she wraps herself around me. "I love you."

"I love you too," she says, kissing me once. Twice. *Three* times. Then she repeats, almost *chants*, "I love you, I love you, I love you."

I chuckle against her lips, realizing, once again, that the world is full of invisible threes... and as the engagement ring burns a proverbial hole in my pocket, I can't help but hope, wish, *pray...*

Maybe third time's a charm...

GUEST LIST

JAKE
MLB PRO

MIKAYLA
MLB WAG

LOGAN
RESIDENT DOCTOR

AMANDA
CHILD PSYCHOLOGIST

CAMERON
ARCHITECT

LUCY
BOOKSTORE OWNER

DYLAN
MAYHEM MOTORS

RILEY
DYLAN'S BOSS

SPECIAL APPEARANCE

HEIDI
RETAIL BUYER

3

Dylan

The best thing about being an uncle is that you get to have all the fun without any of the responsibility. Take now, for example. I'm currently handing my four-year-old nephew two paper plates of whipped cream while we wait for his dad, my brother Eric, to return from the bathroom. Tanner, my nephew, hides under the table while Riley rolls her eyes at my shenanigans. Opposite me, Sydney, Eric's wife, covers her smile behind a Christmas-themed paper napkin.

We're currently sitting around a long table in my mother-in-law's yard, but I have a full view of the back door of my dad's house since the fence between Riley's mom's house and my dad's—where Eric and his family live—no longer exists. It got to where it was falling to pieces, and after a morning spent taking it down, neither of them wanted to replace it. Now they have twice the yard and access to each other whenever they want.

Holly, my mother-in-law, has been hosting Christmas dinner since Riley and I got married, and when I say she goes all out, I mean it. She sets up a marquee tent with heaters to keep us warm and enough decorations to open her own store. Riley once told me that if her mom hadn't gotten into the hair styling business, she likely would have been an event organizer. Which, honestly, made me feel kind of shitty for the way we handled our wedding, but hey, at least she got to help with Eric and Sydney's big day.

"He's coming," I whisper to Tanner, who's sitting silently under the table. The rest of us remain quiet as Eric makes his way over, and I grip the ropes hidden beneath the table nice and tight.

He looks around, then asks, "Where's Tanner?"

I wait a moment for Eric to get comfortable in his seat, then I yank hard on the rope, connected to the back legs of his chair, and don't bother stifling my chuckle as the chair tips. Eric falls backward, his hands going out in front of him, grasping nothing but air.

"Now?" Tanner asks.

"Now, buddy."

Tanner gets out from under the table, slapping the whipped cream plates on his dad's face before sitting square on his chest.

"Dammit, Dylan!" Eric yells while Sydney hands their son a hose.

"Here, baby," she says. "Clean Daddy up."

"Okay!" Tanner exclaims, aiming the hose right at Eric's face, then squeezing the trigger.

I stand, just so I have a better view of Eric shifting his cream-covered face from side to side, sputtering water from his mouth while he attempts to grab the hose from his son. Tanner stops with the water, replaces it with the open bag of flour his mom gives him, then the eggs, then the glitter, because why not?

It's not the most creative act of mayhem, but the kid's four, and we all have to start somewhere, right? Besides, the dog shit I hid throughout Eric's truck is the real mayhem.

"Dammit, Dylan!" Eric yells again, removing a cackling Tanner from his chest. Eric wipes his eyes first, then his mouth.

"You look like Edward from *Twilight*," Sydney giggles.

"If Edward was an unbaked cake," Dad chuckles.

"You wait, D!" Eric threatens, getting to his feet.

I cross my arms, reply, "I'm ready."

"And stop being such a bad influence on my son!" He's trying to sound indignant, but I can hear the slight humor in his tone.

I shake my head. "No can do, big brother. He's a—"

"Don't you dare say it!"

I deepen my voice, make it raspy. "Devil baby!"

Tanner matches my tone. "I'm a devil baby, Daddy."

Eric shakes his head, starts toward his house again. "I'm getting in the shower, and I don't know if I'm coming back!"

"Aww," Dad calls after him. "Who's the baby now?"

With a giggle, Sydney stands. "I should probably go check on him."

"Did I do good?" Tanner asks, the biggest, goofiest smile lighting up his face as he glances around the table for approval.

"You did great, Tanner," I answer, reaching across to high-five him.

He makes his way around the table, parks himself right on my wife's lap. "Was that funny, Aunt Riley?" he asks her.

"So funny," she says, palming his cheek. He leans into her touch, clearly smitten by her. It's no surprise, really. He's a Banks, and all the Banks men love Riley. "But your dad's right," Riley says now. "Your uncle is a bad influence, and you don't always have to listen to him."

I scoff.

Then Bill asks, "How do you even come up with this stuff?"

I shrug. "Years of experience."

Bill is Riley's mom's boyfriend. They met a couple of years after Riley and I got married (when things didn't work out with Logan's dad), and he moved in with her a couple of years later. When he first appeared on the scene, Riley was excited. I was... suspicious. And maybe a little too overprotective. Besides, Holly isn't just Riley's mom; she's mine, too. And fuck if I was going to let some random guy hurt her, or worse, break her damn heart.

So, a few months into their dating, I asked Bill to come on a hunting trip with me and my dad. I figured I'd play nice, then leave his ass in the middle of the woods, never to be seen again.

That *was* the plan.

Turns out, Bill's a great guy. Even Dad thinks so. In fact, I'm pretty sure Bill spends more time hanging with my dad than he does with Holly. Which is fine, it seems, because Sydney spends a lot of time at Holly's, especially since Tanner was born. Sydney claims there are far too many penises at her house, so she likes the reprieve, and Holly absolutely adores her (and Tanner). So, it's a win-win-win for everyone.

As for me and Riley...don't get me wrong; we love our family and love spending time with them, but we also love our little bubble we've created. She works the front desk at Mayhem Motors, and by "work", I mean she gets off her phone or Kindle when the phone rings or a client enters the shop. She doesn't even have to do that, and I'd still want her there. So... we live together, work together, and play together. Personally, I can't get enough of her.

Holly clears her throat now, switching my attention from my wife and nephew to her. She's watching Riley with *that* look in her eyes, and I know what she's thinking before she says the words. "No pressure, but any plans for your own—"

"Mom," Riley cuts in.

I lean back in my chair, ready to take on the world.

Or just Holly.

Kind of the same.

"We already have three dogs," I say, hoping to take the spotlight off Riley.

"Four," Riley corrects.

"Four?" Dad asks, eyebrows drawn in confusion.

"Right," I say, nodding. "Riley brought one home from the pound last night. She says it's my Christmas present."

Dad chuckles.

"I let you name him!" Riley defends.

"What's his name?" Tanner asks.

"Carbo."

"Short for carburetor," explains Riley.

"So, wait," Bill says. "You have Bacon, Cupcake, Wishes, and now... Carbo?"

"That's what she gets for letting me name him," I say, shrugging as I pretend to check my watch. "We should go. We have plans, and we're going to be late."

The goodbyes are fast, with a quick promise to come back tomorrow to raid Holly's fridge for leftovers. Then we start the short walk home. I can tell from the moment we're alone that Riley's mood has dampened. It always does when anyone questions us about having kids, but it seems to be worse when it comes from Holly.

It's not until we're halfway home that either of us speaks. "We're not going to be late," Riley says, and I turn to her. Her cheeks are red, so is her nose, and her lips are darker than they should be. It wasn't as cold out when we left home, and I forgot to remind her to bring a coat. I slow my steps until I've stopped completely, then strip out of mine.

"You don't have to—" she starts, but I'm already wrapping it around her shoulders. I wait as she pushes her arms through the sleeves before taking my time to do up each button.

"I know we're not going to be late," I finally say once I'm done. "I just panicked, I guess."

She nods, taking my arm and holding it to her chest as she resumes our slow pace.

I hesitate to ask, but I know I need to. "I take it you haven't told your mom yet?"

Eyes downcast, Riley shakes her head. "I can't. I don't want to hurt her," she says, her voice shaking with emotion.

I'm not exactly sure which part of our recent experiences she's referring to or what will hurt Holly the most. Either way, I know she's right. So, I don't respond with words. Just actions. I stop in my tracks, forcing her to do the same. And then I just hold her.

"I'm so sorry, Dylan," she cries.

I can barely get the words out through the knot in my throat. "You have nothing to be sorry for."

The moment we get home, I tell Riley, "I'm going to take the dogs for a quick walk, then we'll leave." It's not that I want to get away from her *specifically*. I just need some time alone. As selfish as it is, I need to get lost in my own thoughts, my own feelings, and not have to worry about hers.

Just for a moment.

I leash all four dogs and exit through the garage.

I hope for silence in my mind, but the more I walk, the more painful the thoughts are that fire off inside me. It's one thing for my wife to be hurting, but it's so much worse when she carries the weight of my pain along with hers. She says she doesn't want to talk about it, so I don't know how she feels. But, someday soon, she's going to fall apart. And I don't know if I'll be strong enough to piece her back together.

· · ·

When I get back in the house, Riley's sitting at the kitchen table, her eyes filled with liquid heartache as she stares at the bottle of wine in front of her. I'm quick to get to her—as quick as she is to wipe her tears, hide them from me.

I know my first response should be to check on her, but I check the bottle instead, inspect it closely. "It's sealed," she assures, and my shoulders drop with relief.

Given Riley's history with alcohol, I make sure there isn't even a single drop of it in the house. I have no idea where she got this from, and I don't ask. Instead, I say, "Maybe we shouldn't go tonight."

"Why not?"

"Our friends are going to be drinking, and—"

"I can control myself." She waves a hand toward the bottle I'm still holding. "Obviously."

I look from her dejected eyes to the bottle in my hand, then I empty it into the sink as I stare out the window. The dogs are all out in the yard, Bacon clearly the king of them all. I still remember the look on her face when she first showed him to me. She was working at the animal shelter at the time, and I'd been waiting in the car to pick her up. She was late, and so I went in to get her. She was sitting in front of Bacon's cage, too upset to walk away from him. I barely looked at him the first time, too wrapped up in the news that I was about to be deployed. That I was about to leave her.

She never outright asked, but I knew she wanted to bring him home.

And I said yes, only because I knew she needed something else to focus on while I was gone. Something that wasn't made up of the liquid currently filling our drains.

"Dylan?" Riley says, pulling me from my thoughts.

I drop the bottle into the sink and turn to her. "Yeah?"

She doesn't speak. She doesn't need to. Her eyes give away everything she's feeling. Sadness mainly, but also defeat and fear. Fear that she's disappointed me somehow. It's the last thing she should be feeling. The absolute last thing she needs right now.

I sit down beside her, grab the legs of her chair and spin her to me, scoot her in closer. Then I take her hands in mine, brush my thumb over the rings on her finger—rings that symbolize the life we wanted and the future we spent many nights speaking and dreaming about.

"Will you come with me tomorrow?" she asks.

"Yes."

She cracks the faintest of smiles. "You don't even know where."

"It doesn't matter. I'll go anywhere with you."

Gaze lowered, she says, "I think I should tell my mom."

"Tell her what exactly?"

"The truth."

I nod, release a shaky breath.

The *truth* is harsh and unforgiving.

The truth is painfully agonizing.

The truth is... we *do* want kids.

And we've had them.

Two pregnancies over the past two years, and neither one of them made it past eight weeks.

The first one devastated us.

The second almost destroyed us.

We can't go through that pain again.

We wouldn't be able to survive it.

GUEST LIST

JAKE MIKAYLA
MLB PRO MLB WAG

LOGAN AMANDA
RESIDENT DOCTOR CHILD PSYCHOLOGIST

CAMERON LUCY
ARCHITECT BOOKSTORE OWNER

DYLAN RILEY
MAYHEM MOTORS DYLAN'S BOSS

SPECIAL APPEARANCE

HEIDI
RETAIL BUYER

4

Logan

Ever since Amanda came into my life, she's been the center of my universe. Now, she seems to be the same for around a dozen kids. I can't blame them. Amanda brings the light out of people without ever having to try.

I watch from the doorway as my girl smiles, her eyes getting wider with every word she speaks. She's sitting in a chair in the corner of the hospital's rec room, reading a Christmas story to the kids gathered at her feet. Around the perimeter of the room, parents of said kids watch her work her magic... and that magic is the giant grins and quiet giggles she somehow manages to get out of sick children—children who can't imagine anything worse than being stuck *here* for Christmas.

For their sake, I hope that this is the worst life throws at them. I hope they never have to know about the other kids down the hall, and more so, I hope they never have to *experience* it.

Amanda mock gasps now, motioning toward me as she stands up, saying, "Look, everyone! We have a special visitor."

She's in a red dress with silver tinsel on the hem—a sexy little Mrs. Claus, if you will—and I'm already picturing getting her home and stripping her out of it. On second thought, she can leave it on.

Probably not the best thought to have in a room full of sick children, but I'll never again take for granted how lucky I am to have her.

I push away any illicit thoughts, at least until later, and bellow, "Ho! Ho! Ho!"

"You're not Santa!" a boy yells, and I'm not really sure where he got the idea that I was trying to be, but whatever.

"You're Wolverine!" someone yells from behind me, and I turn toward the voice, instantly recognize him as Caleb—a boy I admitted only hours ago. When I told him my name was Logan, he asked, "Like Wolverine?"

I didn't confirm or deny it, but now I'm Wolverine, and that's pretty fucking cool if you ask me.

Amanda and I hand out presents to the kids in the rec room first, then slowly make our way down the hall to each room of the children's ward. Some parents open their doors or curtains for us, letting us sit with their sick child for a few minutes. Others prefer not to be disturbed, so we hand them the gift if they're willing to accept it and then quickly move along.

This has been our Christmas tradition for a few years now.

Amanda's mom typically visits Amanda's twin brother, Ethan, in Charleston during the holidays, while my dad always volunteers on Christmas Day. Since I want to follow in my dad's footsteps, I volunteer as well. I just finished the day shift, and my dad, who we still live with, is somewhere around here, so Amanda spent most of the day alone. She says she doesn't mind because it allowed her to wrap and label all the gifts we've received from our friends and the community. While I have connections to the hospital, this gift-giving project is *all* Amanda.

And I couldn't love her more for it.

Though, I don't know how she finds the time and energy to do what she does. Outside of her job as a child psychologist, she takes on all these other projects. Earlier in the year, she encouraged people in the town to donate their time and supplies to build a playground at the local church.

We don't even go to church.

"I think this is the most donations you've ever received," I muse.

"It is," she says, her smile all-consuming. There's a skip in her step as she shakes the bag holding the presents. "We even have some left over, so I'll bring them to the shelter tomorrow if you want to come with."

I take her hand, link our fingers. I don't know if I'm doing it to slow her down, or because I need her touch, or just... need *her*.

Amanda seems to know how I'm feeling, because she knows me better than anyone. Better than I know myself. She stops walking immediately, turning to me with her eyebrows drawn in concern. "What's wrong, baby?"

I heave out a breath, attempt to keep my emotions in check. For the last hour, I've gone through the motions. I smiled when warranted, listened when needed, and did my best to hide the blinding ache in my chest. In my soul. But with every step closer we got to *here*, the dread in my gut only amplified. I wouldn't say I'm afraid; I'm just...

I'm reliving a fucking nightmare.

"Logan?" Amanda asks, and I blink hard, force myself back to reality. "Did you just check out on me?"

I lower my gaze so she doesn't see the truth in my eyes. "Yeah, sorry."

"What's going on?"

"There's, uh... there's one more room we need to visit."

"Okay." She nods, looking around. "Where?"

I point over her shoulder to the door with a single window showcasing nothing but darkness. Amanda spins on her heels, and within two steps, she has her palm on the door, ready to push. I stop her with a gentle hand on her forearm and wait for her to face me. "I, uh..." I ignore the widening of her eyes, the confusion bleeding in her stare. Then I rub the back of my neck, no longer able to hide my nerves.

"Logan?"

"Do you mind if I do this one alone?"

It takes a moment for her to respond. For her mind to catch up to my words. "Yeah, of course." She opens the bag of gifts and asks, "Do you know their age and gender?"

I shake my head. "I got this one."

Amanda nods, still uncertain, but she doesn't ask any more questions. She simply smiles, stepping to the side to make room for me. "I'll wait right out here if you need... anything."

What she means is if I need *her*, and I likely will, and she likely knows that already. I press my lips to her forehead, whisper my love for her before pushing open the door.

The room is dark, bar the few lights they keep on twenty-four-seven. Slowly, quietly, I make my way toward him. The boy is nothing but skin and bones, barely taking up space in the bed. His eyes hardly open when I approach—not by choice, but because the bruises and swelling have forced them that way. I don't know if he can see me, but I know he can hear me. "Hey, Micah."

His lips move, just a tad. "I thought you were a doctor."

"Not yet." I refuse to call myself a doctor until I complete my residency.

"Soon though?"

"Yeah... soon."

I can't look at him too long, not in the state that he's in. His chart says he's five, but he's so malnourished, he could pass for years younger.

He's been here for three days now, and his appearance hasn't changed much. Cuts. Bruises. Fucking *burns*.

I was helping Dad transport and admit one of his patients when they wheeled him in through the ER. He was surrounded by so many nurses and doctors and *cops*, and from what I've learned so far, Micah's dad is a real piece of shit. For... reasons, let's just say that motherfucker's lucky he's sitting in jail right now.

The list of injuries on Micah's chart is enough to make a grown man cry. Which I've done. Many times. Usually once his grip on my hand loosens when the drugs in his system have eased his pain long enough to allow him some sleep.

My dad knows I've been visiting with him often. I haven't told Amanda about him. I've tried. I just... I struggle to get the words out.

I clear the emotion from my throat before saying, "I came by earlier to give you a present, but you were asleep."

"A present?" Micah attempts to sit up, but he winces in pain, and I settle my hand on his shoulder, stopping him from moving.

"Don't move too much," I tell him. At the same time, he mumbles, "I've never gotten a present before."

I ignore the weight of his words. For now. But I'm sure they'll replay in my head when I try to fall asleep tonight, just like all our interactions before. "Well," I say, forcing a tiny amount of cheer into my tone. I reach behind the side table, where I hid the bag earlier. Sure, I could've left it for him or had a nurse give it to him. But this is personal, and I wanted to be the one to give it to him. "I'm honored to be the first person to give you one." I reveal the ratty old hat and overused baseball glove from the paper bag and show it to him. "It's not much, but they were mine when I was your age. I figure, once you're better and you're out of here, maybe we could throw the ball around or something."

For a long time, he remains still, and maybe... maybe I overstepped. Maybe I'm doing the one thing my dad told me not to do—get too close to a patient. But then again, if he followed his own rule, *I* wouldn't be here.

After a long moment of silence, Micah finally says, "I don't think my dad would let me do that."

It's not the first time he's mentioned his dad, and it sure as hell won't be the last time I *think* about him. But for now, it's just us, in this room, where no one and nothing can hurt him. Besides, if the justice system is more than *just a system*, Micah will never have to worry about his dad ever again. "Maybe," I say, not wanting to reveal my true disdain for the fucking monster who did this to him. "But we can try, right?"

"I'd like that," he says. "When I'm better."

"Yeah..."

He lifts his head, just a tad. "The hat."

I grab the plain navy-blue hat and gently place it on his head, then crack the tiniest smile when he does. "It suits you."

I swear, he actually *laughs*. It's the faintest of sounds, but it's one I want to bottle and keep in a vial, just like the rainwater Amanda saves. Speaking of Amanda... "Hey, I'd like you to meet someone. Is that okay?"

"Not *another* doctor?"

"No," I say with a chuckle. "Not a doctor."

"Okay."

As promised, Amanda's right outside when I open the door, and she smiles when she sees me, but the concern in her eyes is still present. "All good?"

Not really.

I take her hand in mine, but don't bother answering. I wanted to tell Amanda about Micah first, and then hopefully get a chance to introduce them. But, like I said, I could never find the words. "I want you to meet someone special," I tell her, stopping at the side of the bed and releasing her hand. Then I make my way to the other side so I can watch Amanda's face when I say, "Amanda, this is Micah. Micah, Amanda."

Even in the dull light of the room, I can see the tears that instantly well in her eyes, the way she attempts to blink them away while smiling through her pain. She's seeing him for the first time, and I don't have to imagine how she's feeling. What she's thinking. "Hi, Micah," she says, just above a whisper.

Micah doesn't respond to her, just slowly turns his head in my direction. "She your wife?"

"Not yet," I answer.

"But soon?"

I nod. Laugh once. "Soon."

"She's pretty."

"Trust me. I know it."

Amanda collects the baseball glove sitting beside Micah and inspects it closely. She knows exactly what it is. What it means to me.

"Amanda?" Micah asks, and she replaces the glove before raising her eyebrows and giving him all her attention. "Do you think Santa knows I'm in the hospital?"

Amanda doesn't skip a beat. "Santa knows everything."

Micah sucks in a breath, releases it slowly. "I was just wondering because he couldn't find me last Christmas. Or the year before. Or ever..."

I swallow the ever-present knot in my throat. Sometimes, Micah says these things—gives these little insights into his life —and he has no idea how devastating they are.

When my dad found me, I was so developmentally delayed that I could barely string two words together. I couldn't tell him the parts of my life that still live in my nightmares. Not until I first learned how to speak.

"Maybe I was on the naughty list," Micah adds.

"I'm sure that's not why," I'm quick to say.

"Yeah," Amanda agrees. "I hear sometimes he skips houses when the gift is too big, you know? Like maybe it's one enormous gift that's years in the making..."

Micah doesn't reply. He simply looks between us, his chest rising and falling with each shallow breath. "I know Santa's not real," he admits. "But..."

"But what?" I urge.

"But you are." He lifts his hand, gesturing for me to come closer. I know what he wants, and I offer it to him without a second's hesitation. He holds my large hand in his thin, weak little fingers. "Can you stay with me again? Just until I fall asleep?"

I look up at Amanda, watch for a reaction. She only looks at him when she says, "He can definitely do that."

Micah reaches for her hand, holds it the same way. "And you too?"

"Of course."

It takes less than ten minutes for Micah to fall into a deep sleep, and once he's there, Amanda and I slowly and quietly leave the room.

I expect the questions to come right away, but they don't. Instead, she takes my hand in hers, linking our fingers, and we walk silently, side by side, toward the exit. It's not until we're in the car, with me behind the wheel, that I even attempt to look at her.

She's been crying, as I knew she would be, and a part of me wants to comfort her, but I know she won't accept it, because in her mind, she believes I need to be comforted *more*.

So, instead, I sit with my back against the car door and just watch her. I watch her profile as she stares ahead, each intake of breath more uneven than the last.

I wait, readying the words in my mind for all the things she needs an answer to.

"How long have I known him?"

"How much time have I spent with him?"

"What the fucking fuck happened to him?"

But she doesn't ask any of those things. Instead, she faces me, her eyes red and raw from emotion. "That was the hat and glove your dad gave you when you were—"

"When I was like him?" I finish for her.

Amanda nods once, then blinks, releasing another set of tears.

I shrug, adjusting so I'm facing the windshield again. "It's no big deal."

"Logan..."

"Look, I love you. You know I do. And I know you want to fix this, but this is reality." I think, deep down, this is why I couldn't tell her about Micah. Because as much as Amanda wants to heal the world, nothing we do will change the reality of Micah's life. Or the reality of my past. "These things happen to innocent children every day, and there's nothing we can do about it. I *wish* there was more we could do to help him, but there isn't." And I'm done thinking about it. Done agonizing over it. I need to get the fuck out of here. Out of the hospital and out of my head. "You mind driving home from Cam and Lucy's? I really need a drink... or ten."

GUEST LIST

JAKE
MLB PRO

MIKAYLA
MLB WAG

LOGAN
RESIDENT DOCTOR

AMANDA
CHILD PSYCHOLOGIST

CAMERON
ARCHITECT

LUCY
BOOKSTORE OWNER

DYLAN
MAYHEM MOTORS

RILEY
DYLAN'S BOSS

SPECIAL APPEARANCE

HEIDI
RETAIL BUYER

5

Lucy

It's said that passion dies out the longer people stay together. Personally, I say, *fuck that*. Cam and I have been a couple since we were fifteen, and our physical need for each other has only grown.

Cam had barely put the car in park before I was stripping out of my clothes, preparing myself for whatever he was about to give me. And boy, did he give it to me. Against the front door, on the living room floor, the couch, the bathroom counter, and finally our bedroom. We didn't make it to the actual bed, just the floor, where we currently lie in a heap of sweat and post-orgasm bliss.

Child-free sex is the best sex, and I will die a thousand deaths on that hill.

"I can't feel my legs," I murmur.

Beside me, Cameron chuckles, then leans up on his elbow so he can look down at me. He smiles, his eyes softening as he takes in my appearance. I will never, ever get used to the way he looks at me. The way he worships and reveres me, even when I don't feel worthy of it. "You're so beautiful," he says, running his thumb across my heated cheek. "God, I needed that. Thank you."

"No, no, no," I sigh out. "Thank *you*."

His phone dings with a text, and he whips his head up, looking around. "Where the fuck is my phone?"

I try to think back to when he removed his jeans completely. Sometime between the front door and the couch. "I think it's in the living room."

He kisses me once before standing, giving me a full view of his perfect, naked ass and his bare back—still showcasing the marks my fingernails left behind. I close my eyes, remembering the way his body felt on top of mine. The way his biceps bulged beneath my touch every time he thrust into me, slowly at first, and then... "Babe!" I call out. "You got some juice left for round two?"

Cameron rushes in, his eyes wide, jeans back on. *Boo.* "No time," he huffs out, tapping away on his phone.

I stifle my disappointment, but don't make a move to get up. I'm way too exhausted. Thankfully, my husband knows me well, and he's already opening the dresser drawer to get me a bra and underwear.

"That was Jake," he tells me. "They'll be here in five, but he said they might not stay long because Micky's not feeling great."

I pop my head up just enough to watch him move to the closet. "She's sick?"

He shrugs. "I don't know."

"Ask him."

"Absolutely not."

"What? *Why*?"

"Because it's weird."

I scoff. "What's weird?"

"Men don't ask for details."

I sit up, confused. "What do you mean, *men don't ask for details?*"

He's in our closet now, slipping on a shirt before rifling through a bag in the corner of the closet floor. "We just don't talk about shit. You know Will at work?"

"Yeah, what about him?"

"He got married a few months ago."

My eyes narrow. "Did we not get invited to the wedding?"

"I guess not."

"Why not?"

"Don't care. Didn't ask. Anyway, they got annulled like two weeks later."

"*Why?*"

"Don't know. Because *men don't ask for details.*" He turns to me, holding up something he clearly purchased without my knowledge. "Put this on."

"Wait." I hold up my hands between us, still trying to wrap my head around everything. I don't know what I'm confused about the most. The part where a guy he works with got married and unmarried in the space of two weeks or the giant grin on his face as he pulls a *bush costume* out of its plastic wrapping. "Yeah... I'm going to need details," I mumble.

"Whatever. Just put this on first."

I roll my eyes, but don't argue. I simply find something suitable to wear under the costume and don't ask questions. Besides, I love it when Cameron gets excited like this. When he gets to let loose and act like the carefree boy I fell in love with and not always be the man constantly worried about whether he's doing enough to take care of his family.

"Fits perfectly," I say, viewing my reflection in the mirror. I look ridiculous, covered head to toe in *leaves,* but the pure joy on Cam's face makes it worth it.

Cam settles his hands on my waist. "Goddamn, you're sexy."

I bust out a giggle and turn in his arms. "I'm far from it, but I'm glad you think so."

His grin only gets wider as he takes my hand, leads me to the laundry, where an array of guns awaits us. Not real ones, obviously, but a paintball gun, BB gun, and the biggest, baddest water pistol I've ever seen. I sniff, trying to find the source of the putrid scent wafting through the air. Then I smell the end of the water pistol. "Tuna brine?" I ask.

He pats the top of my head. "I love how well you know me." Then he reaches into the laundry sink for a tiny water pistol and hands it to me. "This one is yours."

It fits in the palm of my hand. "What the fuck am I going to do with this?"

"Go hide in the bushes," he's quick to say, suddenly in a rush. "They'll be here any second." He practically pushes me out of the room, saying, "I'll be up on the roof."

I give him a cheesy thumbs-up. "Got it."

"Who's your target, baby?" he asks.

Shrugging, I assume, "Micky?"

He nods, then pulls a leaf off me and pockets it. "For good luck."

"You're not going to war!" I laugh out.

"Oh, yeah?" he asks. "Remember last year when you had to order and apply fake eyebrows for me because Jake had the boys hold me down so he could *wax* them right off my face? Yeah, baby, it's fucking war."

GUEST LIST

JAKE
MLB PRO

MIKAYLA
MLB WAG

LOGAN
RESIDENT DOCTOR

AMANDA
CHILD PSYCHOLOGIST

CAMERON
ARCHITECT

LUCY
BOOKSTORE OWNER

DYLAN
MAYHEM MOTORS

RILEY
DYLAN'S BOSS

SPECIAL APPEARANCE

HEIDI
RETAIL BUYER

6

Mikayla

There's a stillness about the Preston property that brings a sense of peace, of calm.

Or, at least, it used to.

I'm not exactly sure when things changed.

When *I* changed.

A text comes through on my phone, and I hesitate to check it. As soon as we got in the car to drive here, I sent Mandy, Jake's mom, a message apologizing for not being "myself" earlier. It was the only way I could describe how I've been feeling and acting lately without going into detail. Besides, how do you tell the mother of your boyfriend that her son unintentionally made her question her own self-worth?

I may be experiencing what some might refer to as a mid-life crisis... at the ripe old age of twenty-nine.

Ugh.

After sucking in a breath, I let it out slowly, then read Mandy's reply:

> Oh, sweetheart. We loved spending time with you today and love having you home more. You never have to apologize to us for anything. We LOVE you. And we're always here if you need anything.

A knot forms in my throat at her words, but I'm quick to swallow it down. It's clear, even to me, that there's so much I need. I just don't know exactly *what* it is, and so I don't know how to ask for it.

I've been in my head a lot lately, obviously, and I'm fully aware it's not the best place to be, but I can't seem to escape it.

Jake's parents, Nathan and Mandy, and even his sister, Julie, have been a blessing in my life, and even though I know that, I can't seem to shake these waves of longing that lead to desperation.

I write back:

> I love you too.

Because I do. With everything inside me. And yet, it still doesn't feel like enough.

Blinking back the heat burning behind my eyes, I lower the phone to my lap and glance over at Jake. Shoulders bunched, he has one hand on the steering wheel, the other a fist as it rests on his leg. His brow is furrowed, filled with worry, the same way it is whenever he looks at me lately.

I wish I could fix this.

Fix us.

But I need to somehow fix me first.

Jake must sense my eyes on him, because he glances in my direction, but doesn't say a word.

Within seconds, we're pulling into Cam and Lucy's driveway, the trees surrounding it so familiar, and yet... it's instant... this sudden ache in my chest that's impossible to ignore.

Memories flash through my mind, one after the other, and I close my eyes, try to force them away. The first time I came here was in a limo with a bunch of strangers. It was the night of senior prom. Earlier, I'd been out to dinner with my friends, and I'd caught my boyfriend and best friend together. I fell apart outside the restroom where they'd just had sex, and Jake... Jake was there to pick up the pieces.

I spent the night at *his* prom, with *his* friends, and then we came back *here*, to this cabin, where I spent hours around a campfire by the private lake, getting to know the people who would later become my friends.

I was so carefree then, so *clueless*. I had no idea of the tragedy that awaited me.

That night was the first time Jake and I ever met, and it was the beginning of *our* story. But it was also the end of a huge part of mine. Hours later, when that same limo brought me home, my life... my entire world collapsed and turned into *literal* ash.

I grab Jake's hand, trying hard not to squeeze too tight. I need his touch now as much as I needed it then, and maybe... maybe that's the source of all my problems. I've *always* needed him.

"You okay?" he asks, bringing my hand closer to his chest.

"Yeah," I lie. "I'm fine."

We pull up to the cabin, my hand still enveloped in his. He doesn't cut the engine right away. Instead, he looks at me, directly into my eyes, and forces a smile when he says, "We don't have to stay too long. We can leave whenever you want."

"I'm okay," I say again and force myself to smile back.

He lifts my hand to his mouth, drops a kiss on the inside of my wrist... then quickly all the way up my arm—these open-mouth, sloppy kisses that leave marks along my sweater. He goes all the way to my neck, repeating the action there. I squirm in response, but he has a hold on my arm, keeping me in place, and I *laugh*—loud and unabashed—the sound foreign, even to my own ears.

He pulls back, grinning, as if he's just won a prize, and in a way, he has. The coldness in my chest is replaced with warmth, with love for the man sitting beside me. I reach up, my palm on his neck, fingertips stroking the light curls at his nape. And then I kiss him. The way my heart has wanted to, but my mind could not. He rests his head on my shoulder, a single sigh leaving him. Right before he chuckles.

"What?" I ask, staying close, even when he pulls away.

Shaking his head, his words say, "Nothing," but his eyes... his eyes say *I missed you.*

I missed me, too, I want to tell him, and I'm grateful he was able to get a part of me back, even if it's small, and even if it's only for now.

Jake looks around, his chest rising with his deep inhale. "Hey, if Cam and Luce haven't come out to greet us yet, then that means—"

"Mayhem," I cut in.

He ducks his head, eyes narrowed as he scopes out our surroundings. "They're probably watching us from somewhere we can't see."

"So we have two options," I tell him. "We give them a show, or we get out and take it."

He turns to me, a slight smirk tugging on his lips. "We'll have to get out eventually, but tell me more about this *show* you speak of."

I sit up on my knees, removing the hair tie from around my wrist. Jake's eyebrows shoot up, knowing exactly what I'm suggesting. He watches as I tie up my hair, then turn my entire body toward him. Jake grins from ear to ear, and I pause a second, questioning. "Just to be clear..."

"I know, I know. It's just for show," he responds, flicking on the cab light, then pressing a button on the side of his seat until it's fully reclined.

Without hesitation, I lower my face to his lap and start bobbing up and down.

"Mmm," he hums.

"You know they can't hear you, right?" I say through a giggle.

"I know, it's just you in this position..." He grabs me by the ponytail, guiding me up and down, and I can see the bulge in his jeans growing with each passing second. Then he chuckles. "What the fuck are we doing?"

We lose it. Completely. We laugh together, the silent type of laughter that comes from deep in our chests and has us struggling for air.

"Don't fucking stop," he wheezes out, gripping my hair tighter so he can control my movements, my pace. I picture what we must look like from the outside, and it only makes me laugh harder. "Move your head up more," he tells me. "Make it look like I have a huge one."

I do as he says, inching farther away with each bob. And then I take it one step further, throw in an insane amount of theatrics as I go all the way up until my head hits the roof of the car.

"Okay, now you're just being ridiculous," he laughs, playfully pushing me away, then pulling me back just as fast. For a long moment, he just holds me, my head to his chest, his hand stroking my hair as we let our laughter subside.

It's been a long time since we've connected like this, and I realize now, as I listen to his pulse, his life, beat beneath my cheek... maybe it was never the stillness of the Preston property that brought me a sense of peace, of calm.

Maybe it was Jake all along.

GUEST LIST

JAKE MLB PRO		**MIKAYLA** MLB WAG
LOGAN RESIDENT DOCTOR		**AMANDA** CHILD PSYCHOLOGIST
CAMERON ARCHITECT		**LUCY** BOOKSTORE OWNER
DYLAN MAYHEM MOTORS		**RILEY** DYLAN'S BOSS

SPECIAL APPEARANCE

HEIDI
RETAIL BUYER

7

Mikayla

"You should get out first," I tell Jake. "I'll wait in the car. Just in case."

Jake groans, then squares his shoulders, as if preparing for battle. The second he steps out of the car, he gets blasted with paint pellets, one after the other. I wince, then giggle as I look around, trying to find the gunman... or *gunmen*. They're nowhere to be seen. "Fuck you!" Jake yells, spinning in circles as if that's somehow going to stop the assault. The attack only lasts seconds—ten at most—but when it's over, my boyfriend, along with his dad's car, is dotted in green. There's barely a moment of reprieve before a new set of shots sounds through the air, and now Jake is just outside the car running around, changing directions every few feet. Confused, I get up on my knees to see what the hell is happening. The shots ring out first, followed immediately by the plumes of dirt that rise from around Jake's feet. He *squeals* every time a BB pellet almost gets him and hops from foot to foot. I bust out a giggle, watching his dramatic ass trying to dodge each shot. And, suddenly, the sounds stop. Jake looks up into the darkness of the night. "Reveal yourself!" he demands, and it only makes me laugh harder. He points toward the cabin. "You motherfucker!"

Cam, in all black, is standing on the roof, his arms up in surrender. "I'm coming down," he calls out, waving a white flag.

"You're surrendering?" Jake yells. "I haven't done shit to you!"

Cam disappears from the roof, and Jake takes the opportunity to open the back door, retrieve a bucket of water balloons I hadn't even known were there. Cam's guns vs. Jake's balloons might seem like a dumb move on Jake's end, but he's a *professional pitcher*. My man doesn't miss. Now Dylan with a gun and Jake with balloons—that's a matchup. Jake uses the back door as a shield, ducking just above the window so he can see Cam approaching. I get up on my knees, scoping the area with him. "Good looking out, baby," he says, and I can't help but smile. For seconds that feel like hours, we wait, and wait, and wait. There are no sightings of Cam, or even Lucy. No sounds. Nothing. Then I check the rearview and gasp, "Behind you!" But I'm too late. Cam already has his mark, and Jake spins to him, getting a stream of liquid directly to his face. The smell is instant. *Tuna*. And Jake gags at the stench but doesn't back down. The first balloon hits Cam square in the face, splattering red all over him. Oh, so *not* water. Noted. Cam doesn't even have time to react before Jake hits him with another to the chest. This one yellow.

Ketchup and—

"Mustaaaaaaaaaard!" Cam bellows, and then they're off into the surrounding woods—Jake with his bucket and Cam with his super soaker, roars of laughter shared between them.

A tap, tap, tapping at my window has me slowly, cautiously, facing it. Lucy stands just outside, covered head to toe in fake leaves, holding the tiniest water pistol I've ever seen. "Pew-pew, motherfucker."

I get out of the car, snickering, and immediately wrap my arms around her. "What the hell are you wearing?"

"Cam got it, asked me to wear it." She shrugs. "You know what they say. Happy husband, *crazy* cunnilingus."

"Oh, my god," I laugh out.

"You're supposed to be my target, but I got distracted reading on my phone. So anyway." She attempts to squirt me in the face with her joke of a water pistol. It's so small, so weak, that all it does is leak water from the nozzle. "Pew-pew."

Shaking my head, I open the trunk to retrieve Katie's present and a bottle of wine, then walk arm in arm toward the cabin. "How long do you think they're going to be out there?" I ask.

"Until they run out of ammo."

We make it to the porch steps when a car pulls up. Amanda's behind the wheel of Logan's car, and so we stop, wait for them to join us. Logan approaches first, with a six-pack in each hand, two beers already gone. "What the hell are you wearing?"

Lucy giggles, and I answer for her. "It's for the cunnilingus."

"Makes sense," he says, nodding and looking around. "Where are the guys?"

"In the woods," Lucy answers.

"Right."

Logan waits for Amanda to join him, and after quick greetings, we enter the warmth of the cabin, one after the other. I take their gift for Katie and mine and set them under the Christmas tree, while Logan parks himself on the couch. He's quick to crack open another beer and down half the bottle in a single sip. I glance over at Amanda, who offers a sad smile. Then motion to the kitchen, where Lucy's dumping a bag of chips into a bowl.

Amanda and I join her and huddle close together. I ask, motioning toward Logan, "Is he okay?"

"I don't know," Amanda replies. "We spent the day at the hospital again, and... he's had a rough few days."

I pout. "And you? How are you?"

"I'm good. I just wish there was more I could do for him."

Lucy pulls away, taking a giant store-bought cookie from a paper bag. Without a word, she hides the cookie behind her back and makes her way over to Logan, who's staring off into space, the contents of the beer he opened only seconds ago completely gone. Lucy doesn't speak, doesn't ask him questions. She simply sits sideways on his lap, her legs folded beneath her. She looks like a child against Logan—like a little baby bush he just bought at Home Depot to plant in his yard.

"How you doing, Lucy-Lu?" he mumbles, resting his head on the back of the couch.

She doesn't reply, just offers the cookie to him. His smile is immediate. So is the way his shoulders relax. He takes it from her, but doesn't eat it right away. Instead, he runs his hand up and down her back, the way a brother would console his little sister. Logan and Lucy have always been close, their friendship deep and long-lasting. I can't remember their story in its entirety. I just know that it started with a cookie. It's kind of fitting that it continues the same way. I glance over at Amanda, who watches them, not an ounce of jealousy or even questioning. There's only concern for the man she loves.

Jake often looks at me the same way.

We hear them before we see them, their voices loud. "At least I didn't have to get my brother-in-law to build me a shelf for my *participation* trophies," Jake cracks.

"Your hairline's so far back you salute with your hand behind your head."

"Yeah, well, your face looks vacuum sealed!"

"Funny. Your mom didn't seem to have a problem riding my face last night."

The front door bursts open, and Jake turns to Cameron, his

hand to his chest in mock horror. "You leave Mandy out of this!"

Beside me, Amanda makes a show of sniffing the air. "Why does it smell like tuna casserole?"

Cameron chuckles, then looks around before clapping his hands and shrieking, "Logan's here!" He practically skips toward the couch and makes quick work of removing Lucy from Logan's lap, then taking her spot. Both legs over Logan's, he pats Logan's head. Or, at least, that's what it looks like. It's not until the egg yolk oozes down Logan's forehead that I realize what's happening.

Where the hell did he get the egg from?

Eyes closed, Logan grips his beer tighter and murmurs, "You fucker."

"Clear it," Jake calls, and Cam leans back, giving Jake the line of sight he needs to pitch an egg directly at Logan's chest.

"Oof," Logan winces, smearing the egg on his sweatshirt as he rubs at the spot. "That one fucking hurt."

Now it's Jake's turn to skip over to the couch, singing, "Yay! Logan's here!" He sits on the other side of Logan, lifting his legs over Cameron's.

Amanda giggles. "Idiots," she mutters, just as Cam smashes another egg on Logan's head.

He rubs it in this time, ruffling Logan's hair when he asks, in a tone used for a kid, "How you doing there, buddy?"

Again, *where are they getting these eggs?*

Logan cracks a smile, only one eye open to avoid the yolk streaming down his face. "Good now," he says, pulling his friends in closer. "I got two bad bitches on my lap."

Cam laughs, tells him, "Fuck off," and tries to pull away, but Logan's grip on his shoulder forces him to stay.

The front door opens again, and Dylan and Riley appear.

"Dylan!" Lucy shouts, and we all turn silent. It's a stupid

joke that's gone on for far too long, but we can't seem to shake it.

Riley looks shocked at what she just walked into. Dylan, though? He doesn't seem the slightest bit phased.

The boys all stand, their spines ramrod straight as Dylan approaches them. He looks each one of them up and down—Cam splattered with ketchup and mustard, Jake reeking of fish, and Logan with literal egg on his face. Dylan shakes his head, utters, "Weak."

"Sir, yes, sir!" the other boys say in unison.

"Sorry, sir!" Logan yells.

"Pathetic," Dylan jokes.

Riley places Katie's gift under the tree while Logan finally relaxes and takes his first bite of the cookie.

"You have cookies?" Dylan asks, all excited, his voice filled with childish glee.

Lucy replies, "Just the one for Logan, sorry."

Dylan *pouts*.

"We have cookie dough, I think," Cameron tells him.

"Fuck yeah!" The boys all rush into the kitchen, forcing us girls out of the way. We move to the living room and sit on the floor by the Christmas tree.

"Oh, my god," Riley mumbles, removing her coat. "It took us so long just to come up the driveway. Dylan kept stopping and starting, thinking he was under attack."

Lucy laughs, looking over at the guys in the kitchen. "Nah. They're too scared to mess with the King of Mayhem."

GUEST LIST

JAKE MIKAYLA
MLB PRO — MLB WAG

LOGAN AMANDA
RESIDENT DOCTOR — CHILD PSYCHOLOGIST

CAMERON LUCY
ARCHITECT — BOOKSTORE OWNER

DYLAN RILEY
MAYHEM MOTORS — DYLAN'S BOSS

SPECIAL APPEARANCE

HEIDI
RETAIL BUYER

8

Heidi

Lucy's cabin hasn't changed much in the few years since I've been here. That's not to say that I haven't been home in years; it just means that when I do come home, it's really only for special occasions. The last time I saw my friends was at Katie's birthday party earlier in the year, but that was at the main house. I prefer attending those kinds of celebrations, rather than the closed-wall intimate gatherings that usually take place here.

Throughout high school—unless I could convince my ex, Dylan, otherwise—the cabin was where we spent most of our Friday and Saturday nights. Even then, I felt like an outsider. The boys were Dylan's friends, not mine, and as much as I love Lucy, the things we had in common were very few and far between.

Now we've all grown up, some of us are married, or very close to it, and Cam and Lucy even have a daughter, and I.... I feel like I've grown apart from the rest of them.

Sure, the physical distance doesn't help, but it's not just that.

My connection to all of them was Dylan, and we broke up almost a decade ago. We both moved on. He married Riley, and I...

I honestly don't even know why they *want* to keep me around.

I'm not being self-deprecating, believe me. I'm just... incredibly self-aware of the situation I'm about to walk into. If I felt like an outsider all those years ago while I was *dating* Dylan, you can only imagine how I feel today.

The front of the cabin has enough clearing for at least ten cars, so I find a spot to park that makes for an easy escape. I don't plan on staying long. My headlights shine on the front porch, illuminating Jake and Logan standing opposite each other, their heads bowed, clearly in a deep conversation. They glance in my direction, right before Jake hands Logan something small enough that Logan can shove deep in his jeans pocket. I narrow my eyes, confused, but only for a moment. Anyone who saw the interaction might assume it's a comical drug deal, but considering their professions and the likelihood they'd get drug tested, I'm going to go with some ridiculous form of mayhem.

I step out of the car at the same time Jake and Logan make their way down the porch steps. "Heidi!" Jake greets. "I feel like I haven't seen you in forever."

Logan points to the stain on his chest, then his head. "We'd give you a hug, but..."

I scrunch my nose. "Which one of you smells like tuna?"

"That would be me," Jake answers, and I nod, put on a smile as I pop open my trunk.

"Give me a hand?" I ask, taking out one of Katie's gifts and handing it to Jake. Then another, and another, and another.

"Jeez," Logan says, as I hand him his own stack. "You going for favorite auntie award?"

"Something like that." The truth is, I don't have many

people in my life I buy gifts for, and shopping is probably the one thing I'm actually good at. Since the gang decided to stop doing Christmas gifts for each other a few years back, not even Secret Santa, then the only other people I shop for are my parents. Their gifts are back home, under the Christmas tree, still unopened.

I grab the trays of food I'd spent the afternoon making. I wasn't asked to bring anything; I just... had nothing better to do. And besides, if I was going to be here, I felt it necessary that I contribute *something*.

"Assuming y'all get drug tested, I would probably stay away from the brownies," I quip, juggling the trays in my arms so I can shut the trunk.

"Is it your mom's recipe?" Logan asks.

"Sure is."

"Dang, why you gotta tempt me like this?"

We don't speak as we make our way into the house. No *how are you?* Or *what have you been up to?* I can't be mad about it. I don't ask them either. The second we step into the house, I'm immediately hit with the scent of cookies, most likely still in the oven.

The girls are sitting on the floor, Lucy covered in plastic leaves with only her face exposed. She has a drink in her hand, yelling something heated about what I assume are characters in a book. The other girls argue back, their voices loud and passionate. I'm taken back to my college years, when the girls had weekly book clubs, and I... I wasn't much of a reader.

I'm still not.

"We found a stray," Logan announces, and my chest tightens at his words. I know he didn't mean anything by it, but it's exactly how I feel. How I've felt for years.

Dylan appears from the kitchen, followed closely by Cameron—who's wearing an apron with a picture of a grill that says, "Once you put my meat in your mouth, you're going to want to swallow." He approaches, a giant grin on his face. A second later, I'm enveloped in his arms, and then immediately after, pushed to the side. He smashes an egg directly on Logan's face.

I bust out a giggle as Logan grunts, "Goddamn it!"

The girls greet me the same way—without the egg part, and Lucy says, "We weren't sure if you were going to make it."

Right.

I never actually confirmed I was coming because I didn't know if I was. Meaning, I didn't know if I *wanted* to. Obviously, I don't tell her that. "And miss out on seeing y'all? No way."

Dylan's the last to greet me. Or his version of a greeting, anyway. "Hey, Heids," he says. "I'm going to need to pat you down."

"*What*?"

Beside him, Riley sighs. "Nothing has happened to him yet," she explains. "So now he's super paranoid."

My eyes widen. "Like I have a bomb strapped to me or something?"

Dylan just shrugs.

Riley says, lifting her hands between us, "I'll be quick."

I remove my coat, hand it to Dylan, then raise my arms in the air and surrender to their request, because what else can I do? And I don't ask why Dylan isn't the one to pat me down—whether it's because he and I have a history or because Riley's female. Either way, it doesn't matter.

While being patted down, I ask Dylan, "They really haven't gotten you yet?"

"We don't fuck with the King of Mayhem," Cam tells me.

"What Cam is really saying is that retaliation's a bitch, and so is he," Lucy says. "He's too scared of Dylan's payback."

Then Logan mumbles out of nowhere, pointing to me and Riley, "Fuck, babe, this reminds me of that one porno we watched—"

"Shut up," Amanda cuts in, rolling her eyes at him.

I giggle, looking over at Logan. It's only now I realize how bloodshot his eyes are. He's clearly been drinking. I assume they all have, besides Riley, of course. And possibly Dylan.

"She's good," Riley announces, then wraps me in her arms.

If I'm being honest with myself, Riley is the reason I'm here. Besides the dozen messages back and forth in the gang's group chat this morning, I didn't receive a single text wishing me a merry Christmas. Not from my friends in Atlanta, and definitely not from my parents. The only phone call I got was from Riley, who said she hopes that I have a great day filled with love (didn't happen) and that hopefully she'll see me tonight.

She was the only reason I got out of bed. It was already midday.

I hug her a little longer than necessary.

Dylan comes next, quick and completely platonic.

"Drink?" Lucy asks.

I nod, answer, "Yes, please." I'm sure as hell going to need it.

GUEST LIST

JAKE MIKAYLA
MLB PRO   MLB WAG

LOGAN AMANDA
RESIDENT DOCTOR   CHILD PSYCHOLOGIST

CAMERON LUCY
ARCHITECT   BOOKSTORE OWNER

DYLAN RILEY
MAYHEM MOTORS   DYLAN'S BOSS

SPECIAL APPEARANCE

HEIDI
RETAIL BUYER

9

Riley

Lucy had spent her entire pregnancy in fear... though, she liked to call it "*superstition*." She often declared that the sooner she prepared for Katie, the higher the chances were that something could go wrong.

She was two weeks out from her due date when Amanda and I, as gently as possible, convinced her to get the necessities. Car seat, crib, bottles, diapers, clothes, etc. We drove an hour out of town to a place where we could get everything all at once.

We spent ten minutes in the store.

Lucy barely looked at what she was buying, just pointed to products after checking their safety rating and told the clerk to "wrap it up."

I didn't understand her fear then.

I get it now.

The only thing she allowed to happen earlier was Cam painting the mural for the baby's bedroom. She told us he'd work on it for hours at a time whenever he got inspired. He wanted it to be perfect for her.

For both of them.

None of us knew what the mural was until the day she went into labor. Logan had a spare key to the cabin, so he used it to let us all in. It was during the MLB offseason, so Jake and Micky just happened to be home. I called Heidi, but she was overseas at the time. She promised to come back the first chance she got.

We wanted to make sure Cam and Lucy had everything they needed when they got home. We had planned to make food and freeze it, clean whatever needed cleaning, just help in any way we could. When we entered, we noticed the car seat, still in its box, in the middle of the living room. Same with all the furniture Lucy had purchased. She hadn't even unpacked them, let alone assembled them. Our first instinct was to do it for them, but we all knew about Lucy's "superstition."

Jake called Cameron, who was incredibly relieved we were there, but also told him that Lucy asked us to wait until she was holding their healthy baby girl in her arms. So that's what we did. On whatever surface of the living room we could occupy, we waited. And waited. And waited. For *fifteen* hours. None of us slept. We couldn't even if we wanted to. And when Cameron finally video called us to show a perfect little Katie in her mother's arms, we were so elated. And relieved. And then we got to work.

Since Lucy had to have an emergency cesarean, she wouldn't be home for days, which gave us time. We worked on making the food first, just in case Cameron ducked home for a break. A few hours after we got the call from Cameron, all six of Lucy's brothers, along with her dad, showed up at the cabin. They were there for the same reason. Only, they had brought furniture with them. Lucy's brothers had surprised them with a handcrafted crib for their baby niece—the most perfect piece of furniture I'd ever seen. It matched the rocking chair that Lucy's mother had used with all seven of them.

"Have you seen it yet?" Lachlan, the youngest Preston, had asked.

"Seen what?" Jake answered.

"The mural? None of us have seen it."

It was only then that we all remembered Cam's secret project. We rushed to Katie's room, and I can't even recall who got there first to open the door, but as soon as we saw it, we all gasped. It was, by far, the most brilliant painting Cameron had ever created. In fact, it's the most beautiful piece of art I've ever laid eyes on.

And as I stare at it now, leaning against the opposite wall, I imagine Cameron standing here, in an empty room, with a blank canvas, his mind and creativity at work. I picture every delicate brushstroke that makes up all the leaves of the trees in the enchanted forest. I wonder how he selected all the different pastel pinks and purples used for the sky and if he drew the deer from memory or had to work off an image. And I wonder if Lucy told him exactly which physical pages from her favorite fairy tales to incorporate into the masterpiece.

I wonder if he felt as afraid as Lucy did.

As afraid as I have felt.

The bedroom door opens, bringing more light into the lamp-lit room. Lucy steps in, closing the door behind her. She tilts her head, eyes soft as they scrutinize mine. "Hey..." Her smile is weak, questioning. "What are you doing in here?"

"Sorry," I say—an automatic response. "I used the bathroom and walked past, and I... I was just admiring her room, I guess."

"Yeah, we're definitely going to miss it."

I nod, pushing off the wall and taking the few steps across the room. I lean in close, gaze focused, finger brushing along the raised paint on a single flower.

"We're taking this entire wall with us," she tells me. "Studs and all, so it doesn't get damaged. I love it too much to let it go." She pauses a beat, then adds, "My brothers are making a frame for it, and we'll put it up in her new room. It's almost three times the size, so..."

I nod again, taking in her words but not knowing how to respond.

The crib is gone now, Katie having outgrown it, and it's replaced with a low-lying house-framed bed that Lucy's brothers also built. There's fake ivy wrapped around the posts and sheer white curtains draped over the top, creating a roof. The entire space is just... beautiful. I rub the fabric between my fingers, saying, "She's really lucky to have you as parents, Luce."

"I hope so," she replies, her voice just above a whisper. Seconds pass, neither of us speaking. The longer we stay that way, the harder it is to fight back my emotions. Suddenly, Lucy's hand lands on my shoulder, and as gently as possible, she forces me to face her.

She's nothing but a blur through my tear-filled eyes and, somehow, without me saying a word, I can tell she *knows*.

"I'm so sorry, Riley," she says, bringing me in for an embrace. I swallow down the sob that's begging to escape. She doesn't speak as she sits on the bed, her back against the wall, patting the spot beside her. I do as she asks and let her take my hand, link our fingers together.

When she's this close, I can smell the alcohol on her breath and emitting from her pores. Or maybe I just *want* to.

Need pulses through my veins, just once. Just enough to tease, to let me know it's there.

For a long moment, Luce and I simply stare at the work of art in front of us.

She's the first to break the silence. "I don't know if I've ever mentioned it to you, or if Dylan's ever told you, but Katie wasn't our first pregnancy."

I turn to her. "She's not?"

Lucy shakes her head, her eyes downcast. "We were in college... on a stupid *break*, when I found out." She hiccups—soft and high-pitched. "The worst part is that I lost her before I even knew she was there. There were a lot of medical complications, before and after, and... Katie, she was never meant to be here. The doctors told me so themselves." She swallows her emotions while I release mine in the form of tears. "I'm not telling you this as some sort of advice for you to keep trying or not lose hope. Cameron and I—we had come to terms with the idea that we'd never have children, so Katie really is a miracle baby. But not everyone is as lucky as us. And that's all it was with us. *Luck.* And everyone's journey, everyone's *loss*, is different, and you cope with it however you need to. I'm just telling you because I want you to know that if you need *anything*, at *any* time, you call me and I'm there."

I sniff back my heartache and roll my head against the wall, settle my head on her shoulder—a simple sign to show my appreciation. "What did *you* do?" I ask. "I mean, how did *you* handle it?"

It takes a moment for her to answer. "The first thing I did was push away the people closest to me, including Cameron."

I sigh, picking at a worn spot on my jeans just for something else to focus on. "That reaction must be human nature, huh?"

"I don't know," Lucy murmurs. "Why? What was the first thing you did?"

"The first time—"

"Shit, Riley," she interrupts. "I'm sorry."

"It's okay," I assure, squeezing her hand. "The first time was a surprise. Initially, we were more afraid than elated, but the more we grasped onto the idea, the more excited we became. It was only a week after the positive test that we... It was *devastating*." It's the first time I've told the story out loud and not just let the emotions of the experience infiltrate my mind. It's a lot easier than I thought it would be, and maybe that's because Lucy's the one comforting me, or maybe it's because she's not as close to the situation as Dylan is. Or as my mom will be. "The second time, we actually *tried* to get pregnant, and... and that one didn't last long either. It only happened a few weeks ago—"

"That recent?" Lucy cuts in.

"Yeah." But that's not even the worst part. "I started bleeding at the shop, but I didn't have the courage to tell Dylan. So, I made an excuse to leave work early, and umm..." I wipe at my tears, now flowing fast and free, and try to breathe through the pain of my admission. "I drove straight to the store and bought two bottles of wine."

Lucy rears back, and I can feel her eyes on me when she asks, "Did you?"

A sob accompanies my head nod. "Dylan came home when I was halfway through one. He emptied it in the sink right away, and I... I brought out the other bottle just before we came here. I didn't have any, but sometimes the hurt is too much, and I... I don't know if I actually *want* to, or if I want to test myself, or if... if maybe I just want the pain of something else to replace this one."

"And you've been hiding these feelings from Dylan?"

It's not a question that needs an answer. She already knows because she did it, too. She pushed away the people closest to her. "I don't think Dylan's dealing with it too well, either. And I think we're both struggling to communicate our emotions."

Light fills the room when the bedroom door opens. Dylan stands in the doorway, his eyes immediately finding mine. "I was looking for..." he trails off when he notices the state of me. Then he looks around the room, from the wall, to the toys, then back to me, putting two and two together.

I wipe the evidence of my heartbreak off my cheeks.

"Riley..." he sighs.

Lucy releases my hand, hugging me before getting off the bed. "Any time. Anywhere," she offers, and then she's gone, closing the door after her.

Without a word, Dylan replaces her spot beside me.

He doesn't speak right away, which is good, because it gives me the time I need to say everything I've been feeling. "I'm sorry for pushing you away," I start. "In my mind... it's almost like if I don't acknowledge it, then it never happened, and I don't think that's the best way to deal with it."

"Is that all you're sorry for?" he asks, and it's not accusatory. It's purely questioning. "Because you *keep* apologizing to me, and I don't know why. Do you believe it's your fault? That *you* made it happen?"

I can't contain my sob when I nod, when I finally admit the most painful truth of them all.

"Riley," he murmurs, holding me to him.

I cry into his chest, let it all out. "It's not just with the pregnancies, but the alcohol, too. I disappointed you."

He pulls away, placing his hand on my jaw, forcing me to look at him. Eyes searching mine, he asks, "Is that how you've been feeling?"

I nod again. "It's so hard to be around you, because I'm so ashamed."

"Baby..." He releases me, shaking his head, more to himself than to me. "I'm sorry you've felt that way and that I didn't pick up on it. I've been so in my head about how I can make things better, that I didn't even realize. You could never disappoint me, Riley. Never. So you relapsed. It happens. That doesn't change anything. And it sure as hell doesn't take away from all the hard work you put into staying sober for *years.*"

I listen to his words, let each one of them sink in and make a home for themselves in my heart, right where he lives.

Dylan rests against the wall again, his eyes unfocused as he stares ahead. "Listen, I could happily spend the rest of my life with just the two of us. I don't *need* us to have kids to feel fulfilled, but... we should talk about it, and if we decide that we still want to have children, then we have options," he says, his voice low. "I found a clinic not far from here that specializes in this kind of stuff. Maybe they can give us some answers. And if having a child naturally isn't in the cards for us, we can go a different route." He lowers his head as he continues. "I was going to ask you first... about talking to Logan, seeing if he or his dad can recommend someone to help us. And then maybe Amanda knows someone we can talk to... *together*... if that's something you think might help."

It's the first time he's spoken about all of this, and maybe that's on me. Maybe he didn't feel like he could share his thoughts with me.

A sudden knot forms in my throat, and I'm quick to swallow it down as I watch him work through his emotions. Right now, I see the child version of him I wanted so badly, but more than that, I see his pain. His need to *fix* things. I'm reminded of the man he became when he knew he was being deployed. How he made sure to take care of everything, so I never had to worry about a single thing while he was gone. He repaired everything in our new house, made sure our finances were in order, and had his friends and family check in on me. He took care of every single aspect of our lives. He took care of *me*. Because every task, every decision he's ever made, has been for *me*.

I hold his face in my hands now, my eyes right on his. Flashbacks of the night before his deployment play havoc in my mind. I had shaved his head in preparation, and for the first time since we got together, I saw the fear in his eyes.

Not for himself.

But for me.

There's never been a time when *I* haven't been his top priority.

All he wants is to protect me from harm. From hurt.

When I'm good, he thrives. But when I'm not... he spirals.

"I promise, from here on out, whichever route we go, we go there together."

"Yeah?" he asks, his eyebrows raised.

I nod. "Talk to Logan." Then I smile for what feels like the first time in forever. "Because I really want a little you running around."

"A little me?" His lips kick up at the corners as he picks me up, settles me over his lap. "A little me..." he repeats. "Yeah. I do like a challenge."

"What? You don't think a little me would be challenging?"

"Nah," he says. "That would be a joy. But a little shit like me..."

I giggle, blocked off by his lips when he kisses me. "I've missed that sound," he murmurs against my lips.

"I've missed it, too," I say, running my tongue along the seam of his lips. He parts his mouth, giving me access, and I deepen the kiss just enough to light a fire inside me.

He pulls back, clearing his throat. "It would be highly inappropriate to fuck you in this room, wouldn't it?"

I don't get a chance to respond, because Lucy yelling has us both looking toward the closed door. "Oh, no. What now?" I laugh out.

Dylan taps my leg, the sign for me to get up. He takes my hand as soon as we're both upright. "To be continued?"

"As soon as we get home."

"Can we leave now?"

I hug his arm to my chest while he opens the door, amplifying Lucy's voice. "Give it, you bitch!"

"Get him, baby!" Cam yells.

We turn the corner into the living room and stop in our tracks. Logan's sitting on the couch, where he's been most of the night, and Lucy is sitting *on his shoulders*, trying to grab the beer that he refuses to let go of. The rest of them are sitting on the floor, a smorgasbord of food that Heidi brought spread out between them.

Lucy almost falls when Logan ducks forward, holding the beer out in front of him. "Let me just finish it!"

"No!" Lucy yells. "She'll be out soon!"

It takes a second for me to realize what's happening, and I'm quick to step forward. "Luce, it's okay," I assure, and everyone freezes, all eyes landing on me. Besides Cam, who's too busy using his hands to shovel mac and cheese directly from the baking tray into his mouth.

Logan clears his throat, looking guilty, even though he has no reason to. "No," he says, offering the beer to Lucy. "I don't need it. It's fine."

"No, really," I promise. "I want you to drink."

"Fuck that," Lucy growls. "And fuck you!" She slaps the top of Logan's head. "Give me the fucking beer."

Dylan chuckles at their antics while Logan drinks as much as he can before Lucy finally manages to take it from him. The contents spill when it leaves his lips, soaking his shirt, then his lap, and then Lucy pours the rest directly over his head.

The room erupts with laughter while Logan just shakes his head, runs a hand over his face, then licks his fingers.

"You're going to need to get that couch steam cleaned," Jake says.

"Nah," Cam replies around a mouthful of food. "We're leaving it here. It's the twins' problem now."

"Seriously, you guys. I *want* you to drink," I whine, taking Dylan's hand again. "I have my strength right here."

"Aww," Lucy coos.

"Only if you're sure," Logan pushes.

"I appreciate you all so much, but yes, I'm sure."

Lucy hands him a fresh beer, just as there's a knock on the door.

No one makes a move to answer it. We just stare at it, confused.

"Are you expecting someone?" Dylan finally asks.

"Who even knocks here?" Jake chimes in.

Another knock, and this time, Dylan opens the door. "Roman!"

I gasp, greet him the same way. "Roman!"

"Roman!" everyone cheers. Everyone but Heidi. I don't think they've seen each other recently.

Roman steps inside, his eyes immediately taking in the state of the room and everyone in it. Cam throws a handful of mac and cheese at Logan's face, distracting him long enough to give Dylan the opportunity to hand Roman an egg that was hidden in a shoe. "For Logan," he says, his voice low enough only Roman can hear.

"Huh?" Roman asks, confused, as he should be.

"Roman!" Lucy squeals, making her way toward us with her arms wide open.

Roman hugs her, saying, "I like your outfit. Are you supposed to be a Christmas tree?"

Lucy gasps, her eyes wide when she pulls away. "Decorate me!"

Roman follows her to the tree, where he puts Katie's present beneath it. The other girls are quick to get up and help Lucy remove baubles and tinsel from the tree and put them on her. Roman walks past Logan, drops the egg on his head, grimacing. "I'm sorry, man."

Logan just shakes his head. "I don't even care anymore."

Roman stands in the middle of the room, surveying the mayhem of his surroundings before sniffing the air. "Um... is something burning?"

Dylan squeals. Actually *squeals*. "My cookies!" Then flails his arms as he rushes toward the kitchen. We all laugh as we watch him open the oven door, just to be greeted with a plume of smoke.

I take Roman's arm, lead him to the couch. "Have you met everyone here?"

He pushes up the sleeves of his sweatshirt, revealing his tattoos. "I think so."

"So... how was your Christmas?"

GUEST LIST

JAKE
MLB PRO

MIKAYLA
MLB WAG

LOGAN
RESIDENT DOCTOR

AMANDA
CHILD PSYCHOLOGIST

CAMERON
ARCHITECT

LUCY
BOOKSTORE OWNER

DYLAN
MAYHEM MOTORS

RILEY
DYLAN'S BOSS

SPECIAL APPEARANCE

HEIDI
RETAIL BUYER

10

Roman

I had absolutely no idea what I was walking into tonight, and to be honest, I'm not disappointed. What appears to be absolute chaos is... exactly what it is. At least, according to Riley's rundown. "I still can't tell if Dylan's actually let his guard down or if he's playing it cool," she says.

"Does Dylan *ever* let his guard down?"

"True."

I've hung out with the same people plenty over the past couple of years and known most of them in one way or another for most of my life.

"So, you spent the day with Juan, right?" Riley asks, bringing my attention from Jake and Logan, in the middle of a dramatic thumb war battle, to the girl beside me.

"Yeah, it was a good time," I answer.

"I like Juan," she says.

I chuckle. "So do I." Juan—as strange as it is considering our fifteen-year age difference and completely opposite upbringings—is my best friend. He's also the closest thing I have to family... besides my sister, Addie, of course, but that's another story.

"Were his kids there?"

I nod. "Wife, kids, parents, in-laws, brothers, sisters, cousins, random strangers." I laugh once. "There was so much food, and they just kept making more and more, and his mom... she kept making me plate after plate, and I was so full, but I couldn't say no to her, so I just kept eating."

Riley giggles.

"Swear, I could barely move by the end. I don't think I can eat for days."

"Well, I'm glad you were around people who love and take care of you." She leans into my side. "You deserve it."

I don't know about that, but I appreciate the sentiment. "How was—" My phone vibrates in my pocket, cutting me off. I already suspect who it is, and because of that, I don't answer it in front of Riley. I take out my phone, hold it up between us, facing away from her and say, "I have to take this. I'll be right back."

She smiles, then rolls her eyes as she looks over at Dylan in the kitchen, who's making a slingshot with Cameron. I assume for the cookies that no doubt resemble rocks now.

Instead of returning the call, I send a text instead:

> I'll be outside.

Then I step out of the house, momentarily freezing when I see Heidi sitting on the porch steps, a glass of wine in one hand, her phone in the other. She looks up when I close the door behind me. "Hey." She smiles. Soft. Sweet. Exactly the way I remember her.

"Hey," I reply, shoving my phone in my pocket.

"It's Roman, right?"

I nod in response, but don't say anything more. I don't

expect her to remember me. It's been over a decade since I'd seen her last, and besides, we didn't exactly run in the same circles.

"So how do you know Cam and Lucy?" she asks, and I realize it's the first time she's ever spoken to me.

"I work with Cam." I take a step forward and lean against the handrail, half turned to her, half looking out at the darkness in front of us.

"You work construction with the Prestons?"

"Yeah." I pause a beat. "Technically, he's my boss. So is Dylan."

Her eyes narrow, confused, and I get it. I would be, too.

"I work four days with the Prestons, two at Mayhem Motors."

"Ohhh..." she drawls, nodding slowly. She brings the glass to her lips, downs two giant gulps, then asks, "So you got kids, huh?"

"*What?*"

She rushes out, "No, I just mean you work a lot." She shakes her head now, laughing to herself. "That was such a weird conclusion to think, let alone say out loud." She looks at her glass as if the wine is at fault, then shrugs, takes another sip.

"No kids," I answer. "I just work a lot." Honestly, working as much as I do keeps me out of trouble. In more ways than one.

"So, you work with Cam and Dylan, and you know the rest of the gang through them?"

I grimace. "Actually, I went to school with them." And *you*, I don't say, but she's quick to put the pieces together.

Eyes wide, she almost gasps, "We went to school together?"

I nod, pushing down my laughter when she covers her face with her hands.

"Oh, my god, I'm so embarrassed."

"No, it's fine," I assure, finally sitting down beside her.

Face still in her hands, she refuses to look at me, even when I tap her leg with mine. "I left when I was sixteen, so..."

Heidi looks up, her blue eyes even brighter against the porch lights. "Oh, so you were just there for two years of high school?"

"Yeah..." I hesitate to add, "And middle and elementary."

Face back in her hands, she shakes it slowly. "I'm the actual worst."

Maybe I shouldn't laugh at her reaction, but I do. And she doesn't seem to mind it. I settle my hand on her back, duck my head so it's closer to hers. "It's fine," I repeat. "It's not like we had the same friends back then."

Heidi peers up at me, just one eye open. "We didn't?"

"No," I assure. "I played baseball with Jake."

"*You did*?" she almost yells.

"But Dylan played basketball, right?" Everyone knows Dylan and Heidi got together sophomore year. From what I understand, they stayed that way until college, when Dylan joined the Marines. He met Riley when he came home on medical, and the rest, as they say, is history.

Heidi groans now, sitting up straight. "Thank you for trying to make me feel better. I appreciate it." She offers a smile that has me pulling away slightly. Heidi Stanford has always been beautiful... in that untouchable kind of way. Even without being Dylan's girl, very few boys had the courage to speak to her, let alone look in her direction. To be honest, it's hard to believe I'm even doing it now.

"You know what it is?" she says, then runs a finger along my arm. "It's the tattoos. I bet you didn't have them in school."

"Actually..."

"No, you didn't!"

I crack a smile. "You're right. I didn't."

Her eye roll makes me want to smile wider. I don't. Instead, I glance toward the door, then back at her, and ask something

I've wanted to since I stepped out and noticed her here. "What are you doing out here?"

After emptying the rest of her glass, she mumbles, "The wheel fell off."

"The *wheel*?"

She sighs, long and loud, her shoulders dropping with the force. "I've been the ninth wheel for a long time, and sometimes I just need to..."

"Fall off?"

Nodding, she rests her back against the siding and faces me completely. "I have to say, I'm glad you *know*-know the guys, otherwise the paranoid part of me would assume that you're here for me."

"Uh..."

"I mean, like, they wanted to set me up with you."

"Oh."

"No offense. I just—"

"*Definitely* don't need help in that department," I cut in.

Her mouth opens, shuts, opens again. For a second, I think I may have said something wrong. "If it makes you feel any better, I never confirmed that I was going to come tonight."

"Same," she says.

"So, technically, the whole *pimping us out to each other* thing is very unlikely."

She taps her temple. "I like the way you think." Her eyes are right on mine for the first time in what might be ever, and the longer she stares, the harder it is to *breathe*. Ridiculous, I know, but it is what it is.

I clear my throat, break the stare. "Riley mentioned you live in Atlanta?"

"Riley mentioned me?"

"She likes to sit in the cars I work on and update me on everything."

"Everything?"

"Let's just say I know way more about reality TV than I should."

She laughs at that, and it does something unfamiliar to my insides.

"So, Atlanta?" I push. "Are you just home for the holidays?"

"Yeah..." She lowers her gaze, toying with a button on her coat. "I wasn't sure if I wanted to, so I told my parents I'd try to make it. I flew in last night to surprise them, and turns out, they surprised *me* by flying to Greece a few days ago."

I hiss in a breath, my face scrunching. "Sucks."

"Yeah, I was kind of in my feels about being alone, and I honestly hadn't planned on coming tonight—"

"Because of the ninth wheel thing?"

"Yep."

"So, what changed your mind?"

"Riley called."

I can't help but smile. She called me, too.

"I figured I spent Christmas Eve alone, and I didn't want to spend Christmas night the same way..."

I *feel* that. I got home from Juan's a few hours ago, showered, then parked my ass on the couch, where I planned to stay for the rest of the night. But the longer I sat there, switching in and out of movies and TV shows, the more my mind wandered, and I kept coming back to one thought—my little sister, Addie. I wondered what she was doing and how she spent the day. She had a new family now, a much better one, but I wondered if she thought of me at some point. A part of me hoped so. But an even bigger part of me hoped I was nothing more than a blip in her past.

I looked around my shitty one-bedroom apartment, no Christmas tree set up, no decorations, no laughter, no *life*. It was a huge contrast to how I'd spent the day, how I hoped Addie had spent hers. I picked up my phone and almost called her, but that would've been a disaster. So, to avoid said disaster, I came here.

"So, I spent the day cooking," Heidi says, pulling me from my thoughts, "and I brought it all here, and—"

"Wait," I cut in. "*You* made all that food in there?"

"Most of it, yeah."

"I'll be right back." I enter the house, go straight to the kitchen, where I grab a plate and make quick work of adding one of everything I presume she made. By the time I rejoin her on the porch steps, I have a heaping pile of food on a plate and absolutely zero room in my stomach. Still, I'll eat it all. If she went through all that effort, I want to show her it's appreciated. And the smile that overcomes her only urges me on.

"That's a hash brownie, by the way," she tells me, and I put it aside for now.

Then I dig in. Deviled eggs first, then some stuffed bread thing. "Holy shit," I murmur around a mouthful of food. "Are you a chef?"

"No!" she laughs out.

I swallow, wipe my mouth with the back of my hand. "Don't laugh. With food like this, you *could* be."

Heidi eyes me sideways, doubtful. "What does your diet consist of?"

I clear my throat, look away. "Meat and potatoes, mainly."

She laughs again.

"But that doesn't discount the fact that your cooking is good. Don't sell yourself short."

"Maybe I should cook for you again."

My pulse kicks up, and I try to come up with a response. Luckily for me, rustling from a nearby brush saves me. I stand when Lucas Preston appears in all black with his brother, "Little" Logan, right behind him. I meet them halfway, the plate still in my hand. Lucas motions to Heidi, his eyes narrowed, questioning.

I turn to Heidi. "Please tell me you can keep a secret?"

She pretends to zip her lips, throw away the key. Speaking of keys, I fish the one out of my pocket and hand it to Lucas.

"Cam's doing it now," Little Logan says, tapping at his phone. Then he notices my plate. "Ooh, brownie!" He's quick to grab it, and I'm just as quick to knock it out of his hand. It falls to the ground unceremoniously.

"No." It's all I say.

And all he needs to know.

We all turn toward the house, wait for our cue. A few seconds later, "Jingle Bells" blasts through the speakers loud enough it rattles the windows.

"Go!" I urge, flicking my wrist.

Lucas and Little Logan run toward Dylan's truck, quickly hopping in and bringing the engine to life. They drive away quickly, not turning on the headlights until they're a good distance away.

Inside the cabin, everyone is yelling for Cam to switch off or turn down the music.

I watch until the taillights disappear completely, and the music cuts out. Then I start back toward Heidi, who waits until I'm close enough to whisper, "Mayhem?"

I nod, confirm. Then offer my hand to her. "Come on," I say, motioning toward the door. "Let's go be lonely, only singles together."

GUEST LIST

JAKE MIKAYLA
MLB PRO   MLB WAG

LOGAN ♥ AMANDA
RESIDENT DOCTOR   CHILD PSYCHOLOGIST

CAMERON ♥ LUCY
ARCHITECT   BOOKSTORE OWNER

DYLAN ♥ RILEY
MAYHEM MOTORS   DYLAN'S BOSS

SPECIAL APPEARANCE

HEIDI
RETAIL BUYER

11

Amanda

Trying to maneuver a two-hundred-pound man-child is tough on any day. Trying to maneuver a two-hundred-pound *drunk* man-child is almost impossible.

"I can walk," Logan slurs.

"I know, baby." He *can* walk, just not necessarily in a straight line.

I throw the towel over my shoulder and guide him toward the door with my arm around his waist.

"Why do you have a towel?" he asks.

"You'll see."

I open the door, and come face to face with Heidi and Roman, who are holding hands.

Logan chuckles. "Nice," he says, hand up to high-five Roman.

I push his arm down at the same time Heidi and Roman release each other. "Excuse him," I say, moving us to the side so they can step in. The cool air hits my cheeks the moment we step out, closing the door behind us. Then I "help" Logan down the steps and toward the side of the house.

"It's fucking cold," he mumbles.

"Yeah?" I pick up the hose, aim right for his face. "You're about to get a hell of a lot colder." Then I pull the trigger.

"What the fuck, Amanda!" he grunts, his hands out, trying to block the stream.

I release the trigger, tell him, "I'm cleaning you up!" Physically, sure, but hopefully a little emotionally, too. It's obvious he's been deep in his feelings tonight, and I can't blame him. I've been the same way. The difference? He's trying to heal through alcohol. Each new beer is like applying another internal Band-Aid. Soon, that's all he'll be—a man made of Band-Aids who never actually heals. "Just stay still, okay?" I tell him, my tone much more soothing. I guide his head lower so I can get a better look at the mess in his hair.

Logan doesn't argue. He just does as I ask, wincing from the icy temperature of the water. His teeth chatter, his entire body overcome with shivers. I work as quickly as possible, then drop the hose and cover his head with the towel to keep him warm. After taking his hand, I lead him toward our car. "Get in the back."

Logan faces me, his smile wide, even when his eyes droop. He unzips his fly.

"No, baby."

"Oh."

Again, he does as I ask while I bring the car to life, put the heat on full blast. Then I get in the back, climb over him and straddle his lap.

He starts to unzip again. "Fuck yeah."

I slap his hand away.

"Oh."

As gently as I can, I dry his hair, hoping the warmth of the heater and the quiet around us create a sense of calm within him. He settles his hands on my thighs, and I listen intently to the way his breathing slows.

"That's nice," he hums. "*You're* nice."

Done with his hair, I grasp his jaw, force him to look up. There are still remnants of egg and whatever other food he's been attacked with tonight, and I use the edge of the towel to wipe off as much as I can. His gaze shifts from my eyes, to my nose, to my mouth, and back again, as if he's searing my face into his memory. In the decade we've been together, he often looks at me that way, as if I'm going to up and vanish one day, and he'll never see me again. Just to be clear, this man is my world.

My life.

My *light*.

"I can't stop thinking about him," I finally admit.

"Who?" he asks, suddenly sitting taller. "Amanda, I'm drunk. I can't be throwing blows with some random guy tonight. I'm going to get my ass kicked."

I shake my head, crack the faintest of smiles. "I meant Micah, you idiot."

"Oh." His shoulders relax, and he rests the back of his head on the seat. "Well, I don't want to throw blows with him." His eyes drift shut, and I know what *I'm* thinking, but Logan—he says it out loud. "He's had enough of that already."

"Do you know who did that to him?" I've been thinking about it all night, but I couldn't find the right time to ask.

"His dad."

My stomach drops. "Where was his mom?"

Logan heaves out a breath before answering, "I suspect six feet underground, considering she's dead."

"And the rest of his family?"

He adjusts both of us until he's more comfortable, a clear sign that he's ready to talk. He may not be in the right state of mind for this conversation, but I'll take what I can. For now.

"The social worker has only been in once to see him. She says she and the cops are trying to find a next of kin, but... it's not looking good."

I set the towel aside and place my hand on his chest, right above his heart. He covers my hand with his, the other going to my face, stroking my cheek with his thumb. He doesn't say anything. He just looks at me, those sad, solemn eyes making me weak. I ask, "What happens once he's better? Where does he go?"

Logan shrugs, dropping his hands to his sides. "Probably a group home."

I suspected as much, but still... "That doesn't seem right."

"That's life, babe."

"So you've said," I whine, my tone harsher than expected. "And you said there's nothing more we can do."

"There isn't," he deadpans.

"Who says?"

"Reality says."

"Why can't he come home with us?" The words are out before I can catch them, but Logan doesn't seem at all surprised by them, as if maybe... maybe he's been thinking the same.

"As much as I love you for thinking of that, and as much as I want to, I'm still doing my residency, and you have clients who need you. The timing—"

"Why can't *he* be my client?" I cut in.

"He can, but that's all he can be."

Tears well in my eyes, and Logan looks away. He can't stand to see me hurt as much as I can't stand to think what Micah's future might be like if we don't do something about it.

Logan adds, still refusing to look at me, "It's not as if we can just sign him out of the hospital and bring him home with us. I'm pretty sure we'd need to be screened by—"

"We would," I inform. I've dealt with this side of things

before with clients of mine. "We'd have to qualify to be foster parents."

"We live with my dad, Amanda. And on paper, we're just a couple in our late twenties. We're not married. We're not even engaged. Those are things that could disqualify us."

"You've thought about it a lot, haven't you?"

"Of course I've thought about it," he admits. "But that's as far as I've gotten."

"Why didn't you tell me about him earlier? Why didn't you come to me?"

"What was I supposed to say? There's this beaten kid at the hospital and he reminds me of me, and I want to take care of him?"

"Exactly that!" I almost cry. *Almost.* Because I didn't just see Micah lying in that hospital bed. I saw *Logan,* too. I saw them hurt and *alone* and desperate for someone to love them and care for them the way they deserve. "Logan, we're a team. What matters to you, matters to me."

"Amanda," he sighs, his eyes meeting mine. He's quick to wipe the tears that cling to my lashes. "It's a lot. We know nothing about him. What if he has developmental or *behavioral* issues? The hours I've spent with him in the hospital might differ completely from what he's like every day."

"And that means he deserves less?"

"You know that's not what I'm saying."

"Then what *are* you saying?"

It takes him a moment to answer, and when he does, the ache in my chest only amplifies. "What if we can't fix him?"

"But what if we can?"

"I can't be home for him twenty-four-seven," he utters.

"But I can," I assure, and I realize I'm pushing the subject harder than I should, especially in the state that he's in, but I can't seem to help it. "I'll change the appointments for my clients when you're home. I'll work around your schedule. That way, he'll have someone with him all the time. You can help him physically, and I can help him emotionally. We're *exactly* who he needs right now." And I don't understand how he can't see that.

"For how long?" he's quick to say. "And when our time's up or they find a family member, what happens to him? Do we just let him go? Is he going to feel unwanted again? And how are *we* supposed to go on being responsible for him feeling that way?"

It's clear now that Logan hasn't just "thought about it" in passing. He's thought about every aspect of it. Aspects I haven't even begun to explore. "I think..." I swallow the knot in my throat, trying to see things from his perspective, but every time I try, all I can picture is Micah in that bed. And then Micah is replaced by the many, many other kids in the same situation.

"You think what?" Logan asks.

Shaking my head, I heave out a breath. "I think this is one of those times where we need to put his safety and feelings before our fears."

For a long moment, he does nothing but search my eyes, as if hoping to find the answers to the many unspoken questions infiltrating his mind. He starts to speak, then hesitates, before dropping his gaze between us. "I worry you would only be doing this for me," he murmurs. "And that something might happen to make you regret this decision, and I'll be at fault." He holds me to him, his embrace gentle yet firm. "I don't want to lose you, Amanda. I *can't*. Not again."

"That won't happen," I try to assure, but I know it means little right now.

"You don't know that." His hold on me loosens, and I pull back so I can watch the million emotions cross his face. "You don't know how messed up I was when my dad found me. You don't know how hard he worked to get me to—" A quiet sob breaks through his strength, and I'm quick to wrap my arms around him. He buries his face in my neck, saying, "I don't want to do this right now."

"Okay." I lace my fingers through his hair, attempting to soothe the parts of him I can't cure. Not with a Band-Aid. Not with my words. Not even with my presence. "We won't do this now, but soon, okay?

"Okay."

For seconds that could be minutes, or minutes that could be hours, we stay exactly how we are. I listen as his breaths slow to a calm and mine do the same, until eventually, our hearts beat as one again.

He pulls away, the back of his head hitting the seat. Then he's searching the darkness around us. Eyes narrowed, he leans forward, looking out the window. "Dylan and Riley were still inside when we left, right?"

I tilt my head, trying to recall. "Yeah."

"And nobody took off while we've been in the car?"

"No." I look out the window, trying to see what he sees. "Why?"

"Where the fuck is his truck?" He faces me, a mixture of confusion and intoxication swirling in his eyes. And then he busts out a laugh. This joyful, beautiful sound that I've missed all night.

It takes a moment for my mind to catch up to his, for clarity to hit. "He's going to be so pissed," I laugh out.

"He's been on edge all night. Jumping at every sound," Logan chuckles, opening the door. "We have to stay to see his reaction."

We're still laughing as we make our way back to the cabin. The second we open the door: eggs. Multiple. Right at Logan's face.

He freezes beside me, his eyes closed, his nose flaring with every harsh exhale. Our friends stifle their chuckles, but I already sense what's going to happen before Logan makes his first move. He smiles, wiping the egg off his eyes. "You mother-fuckers," he deadpans, and then he charges forward. All the boys—aka the culprits—run in the same direction, into the living room, shoving each other out of the way, or in Cameron's case, backward and directly into the path of Logan. Logan takes his chance, jumps on his back, until they're both on the floor, wrestling.

"Get him good, baby," I call, moving to the couch for front-row seats.

The boys are yelling now, telling each of them what moves to make, as if any of them have a single clue. Then Cam suddenly gets a burst of strength to push Logan onto his back. Meanwhile, Lucy sidles up to me, grasping a bottle of wine. She parks her tiny ass right on my lap, saying, "This is very erotic." A sip and a hiccup later, she adds, "I'm getting turned on."

I giggle, hugging her closer.

"Go, Logan!" Lucy shouts, lifting the bottle like a trophy.

Cam sits up, looks at her. "The fuck?"

Logan takes the opportunity to roll out from beneath him, and I catch a glimpse of something on the floor next to him. My eyes narrow, physically zooming in on it, and when I realize what it is, I let out a gasp. I stand, effectively dropping Lucy to the floor with a thud. I offer a half-hearted apology as I take the few steps toward the object, now sparkling under the ceiling light. Slowly, carefully, I pick up the gold band, the diamond setting brilliant and... *huge.*

"Shit," Logan mutters, and I snap my eyes to his. He's sitting up now, his knees raised, arms resting on them. Head between his shoulders, he shakes it slowly. "Amanda..."

I feel like I should be elated or in a daze of some sort, but I'm more curious than anything. "Did this fall out of your pock-et?" I ask, because I highly doubt Cam has a use for it. Lucy's ring is her mother's. She'd never replace it.

Logan looks around as he releases a sigh. "Yes, but it's not for you, baby."

The room is silent. If the house had a clock, its ticking would be the only sound you could hear.

"I'm sorry."

I shake my head. He doesn't need to be sorry. We've spoken about marriage. We agreed to wait until his residency was over, and we were both in a position to plan the rest of our future together. We're not there yet. But if he has the ring, and it's not meant for me, then... "Who's it for then?"

Mikayla steps forward, taking the ring from me. "It's mine."

GUEST LIST

JAKE
MLB PRO

MIKAYLA
MLB WAG

LOGAN
RESIDENT DOCTOR

AMANDA
CHILD PSYCHOLOGIST

CAMERON
ARCHITECT

LUCY
BOOKSTORE OWNER

DYLAN
MAYHEM MOTORS

RILEY
DYLAN'S BOSS

SPECIAL APPEARANCE

HEIDI
RETAIL BUYER

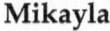

12

Mikayla

"Wait." Lucy picks herself up off the floor. "How do you know it's yours?"

I inspect the ring closer, just to be sure. "Because I've seen it before."

"When?" Amanda asks.

"When I've proposed before," Jake answers for me, resting his shoulder against a wall. His eyes are downcast, refusing to look at me.

"And you said no?" Riley asks.

I don't respond, so again, Jake does it for me. "Twice."

The girls gasp, but the boys... the boys don't seem at all surprised by the news.

"It was only *once*," I retort, and it's ridiculous to get into the semantics of things, especially now, but the pressure of everyone's eyes on me feels like a weight pressing down on my chest.

The girls start with the questions, all of them, all at once, and as if planned, their boys cover their mouths, shrouding the room in silence again. My shame and insecurities have prevented me from telling anyone about the proposal, but I understand why Jake needed to talk to someone about it. Or multiple *someones* based on the guys' reactions. They know, and they kept it from their girls for what? To protect Jake? To protect *me*? I turn to Jake and speak to him, and only him. "You asked me if I wanted to when we were in college, and I said *not yet*. That's not a proposal."

"Fair," Jake responds, pushing off the wall to stand taller. "But I waited years to propose, and you said the same thing. I don't live in your head, Kayla. I don't know when the right time is, but we've been together for ten years now, and we're exactly where we started." There's no bite in his words. No fight. Just *facts*.

I look around the room at our friends, all of them waiting for answers, and I don't want to be having this conversation. Not now. Not with an audience.

Roman covers Heidi's mouth, and she's quick to pull down on his arm. "I wasn't going to say anything," she tells him.

He shrugs. "I just wanted to fit in."

"Why didn't you tell us?" Lucy asks, the hurt in her voice unmistakable. Tears form in her eyes that bring on my own, and I wish the world would swallow me whole. I'm aware how amazing my friends are, how they would swoop in at the drop of a hat to be there for me, but if I can't reveal my feelings to Jake, then how am I supposed to do it with them? And believe me, I *know* how this looks from the outside—like I'm purposely keeping secrets from the people who care about me the most. Or like I'm not committed to Jake as much as he is to me. But that's not what this is. It's not even close. "You guys..." I cry, a single tear losing its battle to hold strong. "It's not that I don't want to marry Jake, It's..." How do I even begin to explain the emotions I've been drowning in for far too long?

Heidi's tone is understanding, not judgmental, when she asks, "It's what?"

I wipe at my tears, focusing on everyone's eyes on mine, then slowly turn to Jake. His stare is empty, void of the emotion he's been carrying lately. I know, deep in my heart, in my gut, if I don't open up soon, I'll lose him. And that, to me, is a fate far worse than death. I approach him, sniffing back my heartbreak. "Can we talk?" I ask, motioning to the door. "Outside maybe?"

"Great idea! Give us one minute." Amanda chimes in.

I shake my head. "I meant just me and Jake."

"I know." She holds up a finger. "One minute. Maybe two."

Confused, I stand by Jake as our friends huddle together, their heads bowed to the middle, whispering words too quiet to hear. After a moment, Amanda yells, "Ready?"

The rest of the gang clap once and shout, "Break!"

And then they're off, rushing in all different directions, gathering... supplies, I guess? I don't really know, and honestly, I'm too deep in my own head to try to figure it out.

Dylan stands by us, his stance wide, arms crossed. "I'm supposed to be making sure you don't move."

I hadn't planned to.

Once the commotion ends, Amanda enters the living room and takes my hand in hers. "It's ready."

"What's ready?"

She doesn't answer, just hands me and Jake our coats and waits patiently for us to slip them on. Then she leads us out to the front porch, where everyone else is waiting. In the space of a few minutes, they've gathered Katie's mattress and placed it on the porch, along with some blankets, a portable heater, food, wine and even hot chocolate.

"You have no excuses now," Amanda tells us. "So take your time."

I face her. "You're a therapist twenty-four-seven, huh?"

She shrugs, smiling proudly. "Can't help it."

"Try living with her," Logan mumbles, and the glare Amanda throws his way is enough to set the entire cabin ablaze. Logan grins from ear to ear, switching his tone. "It's the best!"

"Get your ass inside," Amanda orders.

"Yes, ma'am."

They all file back into the house, one by one, leaving me and Jake alone. I turn to him, try to offer a smile, but surely fail. There are so many things I've wanted to say to him, and it's not as if I haven't tried before. I have. But it's so hard to put myself back in the moments and memories that have made me like this.

He sits on the mattress, his back against the cabin siding, and picks up a hot chocolate. "Come on," he says, motioning for me to sit beside him.

I do as he asks, grabbing the blankets and carefully placing them over our laps. He hands me the warm drink, then grabs his own. For a long moment, we do nothing but sip and stare out at the darkness in front of us, and I find myself in the same predicament I always do whenever these quiet moments fall between us —so much I want to say, but I don't know where to start. I decide to start with tonight and hopefully work my way back. After clearing my throat, I ask, "You were going to propose to me tonight?"

Jake practically downs his hot chocolate, putting the mug aside before answering, "No."

I lift the ring up between us. "Then why is this here?"

"Because I've been carrying it with me everywhere since the last time I asked you."

I turn to him. Not just my head, but my entire body.

"I figured it would just happen, you know? Like, I'd know *the* right moment... the right time and place to ask again." He says all this while keeping his eyes forward, never once looking at me.

Voice as weak as my heart, I whisper, "Jake..."

"I gave it to Logan tonight because..." He laughs once, not from humor, but more disbelief. "I guess the athlete's superstition kicked in. I thought maybe the ring was the reason that *moment* hadn't happened yet. Or..." he trails off.

"Or what?" I push.

"I don't know. Maybe that ring is the reason I feel you pulling away. And it's only gotten worse since we moved to St. Louis." He turns to me, those deep blue eyes I fell so in love with now filled with nothing but questions. "I keep trying to pinpoint the exact moment things changed. We moved there and everything was great, and then halfway through the season, you just... I don't know..."

I do.

"Did something happen, Kayla?"

I try to pull away, my go-to move it seems, but he's quick to grab my arm.

"What happened?" he urges.

"It's nothing, Jake. It's *so* dumb." I roll my eyes at myself, ignoring the heat burning behind them. "And so pathetic." And the reason I could never find the courage to tell him.

"Tell me, anyway," he asks. "*Please.*"

My vision blurs, caused by my tears, and my breaths falter. Jake pulls me in closer, lifting my legs and dragging them over his so we're as close as we can be.

Even as I prepare the words in my mind, I realize how ridiculous it will sound. "You know how I used to sit in the suite with all the other wives and girlfriends?"

His eyes search mine, as if trying to find the end of the story within them. "Yeah?"

I drop my gaze. My voice, too. "I was running late one day, and I came in when everyone was already there, and I overheard them talking about me."

"What the fuck did they say?" Jake spits, the harshness in his tone palpable.

"Nothing *bad*," I try to assure, because I don't want him to think he's at fault. He's not. But to this day, I can still remember the things that were said, and more importantly, the *way* in which they said them.

"He took her in when her entire family was murdered and her house was set on fire."

"They were strangers. They literally met the night it happened."

"She's been living with him ever since."

"She doesn't work, doesn't do anything."

"She's earned nothing for herself."

"She's been leeching off him since they were eighteen."

"Freeloader."

"Gold digger."

"The poor guy. He couldn't leave her, even if he wanted to."

Whenever someone asks how Jake and I met, I tell them about the dinner before senior prom, the dance, and Lucy's cabin afterward. I leave out what happened next because reliving it brings on too much pain. Too much anguish. I don't expect Jake to feel the same, so how *he* tells people is up to him. And how people interpret that is on them.

After listening to my life being torn to pieces, to my pride being ripped apart, I couldn't speak. Couldn't move. Then one of them turned and saw me, and then the others did, too. They were surprised to see me, but they weren't sorry. Even now, not a single one of them has apologized.

I don't know if they said anything else after they realized I was there. I just remember how it *felt*. Like the life I'd built and the world I'd created meant *nothing*, and as I stood there, I felt it all crash down around me.

I've never thought of myself as a weak person, or even insecure, but I felt it then, and I've been feeling it ever since.

I finally walked away, furious at myself for not speaking up.

For not standing up for myself. I knew that if I was with my girls, Lucy would have cursed them all to hell. Amanda would've slapped at least two of them, and Heidi—Heidi would've really gotten to them by calling out their fake designer bags. But... I was alone. And I never felt it more than I did then. I didn't cry at that moment, but I do whenever I think back on it.

"I think it's part of the reason I come back here so much," I tell Jake after explaining that day to him. "I think I wanted to be closer to my friends, but then the insecurities kick in, and I think... what if they see me the same way? I know it's not true, but I can't help but wonder. And the more time that passes, the more I've started seeing myself and my life through the eyes of those women."

Jake hasn't spoken once since I started talking, but I know he's listening to every word, every piece of my heartache.

"It's embarrassing," I finally admit. "I'm close to thirty, and I have nothing to show for it besides you. Those girls were right. I've barely worked a day in my life, and I've not *earned* anything for myself."

Jake finally speaks up. "You've been supporting me and my dreams."

"That's not how other people see it."

"Who fucking cares what other people think?"

"I do, apparently."

"Babe..." He forces me to look at him, right into his eyes. The questions still linger there, but most of all, I find strength in his stare, courage in the way he embraces me. Ten years on, and it feels the same as it did the first time he held me like this —when I stood outside my childhood home and watched it all disintegrate. "Firstly, your reaction to what they said isn't dumb or pathetic. They are. They don't know your strength or the will it takes to overcome what you have. Fuck them. They're wrong. And they know it, too, because none of my teammates have told me about this, which means their partners didn't tell them, and you know why? Because they're fucking ashamed of themselves, as they should be. But that shame is theirs to carry, Kayla. It's not yours. And if I have to spend the rest of my life proving that to you, then I will."

I blink away the tears that fade with each of his words. "The rest of your life, huh?"

He tenses momentarily, already knowing where I'm going with this.

"Even if we're not married?"

Jake sighs, long and almost silent. "You know I love you, right?"

I nod, positive. "You prove it every day."

"And I know you love me," he says.

"Our love is the only thing in this world I'm sure of."

"So... you just don't want to get married at all? Is that it?"

It's the first time he's asked so directly, and also the first time I've felt comfortable enough to answer in truth. Every heartbreaking ounce of it. I lean closer into him, rest my head on his shoulder. "Do you remember Cam and Lucy's wedding?"

Jake sucks in a breath, releases it slowly. "It goes that far back?"

I nod. "When Lucy was getting ready to throw her bouquet, Amanda and I exchanged some fighting words. We were so ready to tackle each other for it. But then when it came time, I ran away..." I pause a breath, trying to form words that bring sense to my thoughts. "I feel like I've been doing that ever since... *running away*. I didn't understand it then—why I was so afraid of the prospect of a wedding, and when you brought it up the first time, I opened my mouth to say yes, but then... then this image flashed in my mind of our wedding day." A knot forms in my throat, but I manage to push through. "My mom and sister were there helping me get ready, and my dad... he was so excited to walk me down the aisle." I release a sob, along with my tears, and I look up at the man who's always there to wipe them away, just like he does now. "The thing is... they were the versions of themselves that I last knew, that I last touched and held, and I've aged since then, but they... they haven't. They're stuck in time, and they're never going to grow with me, and in my head and in my heart, my sister's still eight years old. She'd be nineteen now, off at college, and I know it's not my fault—what happened to them, but..." My heartache is too much, too overwhelming, too painful. "Who's going to walk me down the aisle, Jake?" I cry. "Or go dress shopping with me? Or..." I trail off, no longer able to speak through my sobs.

Jake's pain *for* me gets the better of him, too. He holds me to him, sniffing back his emotions as he strokes my hair. "I'm sorry," he whispers, dropping a kiss on my forehead. "I should've picked up on your feelings."

"No." I shake my head, peer up at him through glassy eyes. "I should have told you. It just..."

"It's hurts too much?"

I nod.

He kisses me again, his lips warm against my temple.

For a long moment, we stay that way, his mouth pressed to my skin, his love forever etched in my heart. Eventually, he pulls away, his eyes right on mine when he says, "Kayla..." It's just my name. He's said it a million times before. But this time, it holds a myriad of meanings. "I have everything I've ever wanted in my life, and I could lose almost all of it tomorrow and still be happy. As long as I have you, my friends, and my family, that's all I *need*. But what I *want* is for you to be my *wife*."

"Jake..."

"When I've proposed to you before, I wasn't asking for a *wedding*." He takes the ring I'm still grasping on to and slides it on the correct finger. No question on his end. No rejection on mine. "I'm asking you to *marry me*."

I find myself smiling as I look down at the ring on my

finger, feeling whole for the first time in what seems like forever, and that smile only widens when I look up at my future husband. "Come on," I say, grabbing his hand and getting to my feet.

Like the "proposal" that just occurred, Jake doesn't ask questions.

I open the cabin door, only to be met with the silence of an empty living room. "Hello?" I call out.

"We're in here!" Lucy responds from somewhere down the hall.

Still holding Jake's hand, our fingers entwined, I check Cam and Lucy's bedroom first. Empty. Then I check Katie's. All eight of our friends are huddled in the tiny room, a white noise machine blasting from the corner. They all look up, eyes wide, expectant.

"What are you guys doing?" I ask.

Amanda answers, "We didn't want to accidentally overhear anything, so..."

"She's wearing the ring!" Logan announces, his grin from ear to ear. His excitement sparks the rest of them and also sparks something deep inside me.

I hold up my hand, show off the symbol of Jake's eternal love for me. "Who's in the mood for a wedding?"

Lucy squeals.

Everyone moves, ready to congratulate us. "Oh, my god," Amanda sings, taking my ring-adorned hand in hers. "We have so much planning to do!"

"And you have about an hour to do it."

Everyone freezes, all attention on me.

"*What*?" Heidi asks.

"We're getting married. Right now."

"*Now*?" Jake asks.

I look up at him, biting my lip, unsure. Truth is, the moment his earlier words fell from his lips and into my heart, and the ring was on my finger, everything felt so, *so* right. I didn't want to wait a second longer, but maybe... "You said..."

His smile grows with every second of our stare until it forms completely. And then I'm in his arms—an embrace so strong it knocks the air out of me. "Let's get married."

The celebratory shouts last all of a second before Amanda yells, "Dylan!"

Silence.

"Lucy, you help me set up," she orders. "We'll do it out on the dock."

"The dock is freezing," Lucy mutters.

"We have coats!" Amanda yells, and I giggle into Jake's arm as I hold it to my chest.

"Okay, Amanda the Demander," Lucy replies, holding her hands up and side-eyeing our friend. "Jeez."

"And besides, we need an aisle at least," Amanda says, calming her tone and offering a weak, somewhat apologetic smile. "And it'll take ten minutes. Anyone can do anything for ten minutes!"

Logan pipes up. "I'll remember that next time you're sucking my di—" He doesn't have time to finish before Dylan has him in a chokehold from behind while covering his mouth.

"Shhh," Dylan whispers in his ear as Logan pretends to go limp in his arms. Dylan drags him out of the room, saying, "That's it. Relax and it'll be over soon." Dylan waits until he's in the hallway to drop Logan like a bag of rocks, and Logan lands to the floor with a dull thud. He doesn't move from there. Doesn't even open his eyes.

"I'll be right back," Amanda rushes out. None of us speak; we merely wait, eying each other. She returns seconds later with one of Cameron's suits and slams it against Jake's chest. "You can't get married smelling like fish." She turns to Lucy. "I accidentally knocked over your box of sex toys. Sorry." Then she points to Heidi, smiling. "You! Help her look like a bride!"

Heidi nods once. "On it, boss."

"Cam, Dylan, you're in charge of the cake!"

"What about me?" Logan asks, still playing dead in the hallway.

"You... get a speech ready. You'll officiate the wedding!"

Lucy hiccups, and Amanda glares at her, then everyone else. "Why are you all still standing around?" She shoos us away with her hands. "Go, go, go!"

GUEST LIST

JAKE
MLB PRO

MIKAYLA
MLB WAG

LOGAN
RESIDENT DOCTOR

AMANDA
CHILD PSYCHOLOGIST

CAMERON
ARCHITECT

LUCY
BOOKSTORE OWNER

DYLAN
MAYHEM MOTORS

RILEY
DYLAN'S BOSS

SPECIAL APPEARANCE

HEIDI
RETAIL BUYER

13

Cameron

"Are you sure it's okay we're here?" Dylan whispers, hopping off the golf cart as quietly as possible. Thankfully, I was able to corral him out of the cabin through the back door, so he didn't notice that his beloved truck is still missing.

"Yes," I whisper back, glaring at Logan behind me who thinks *now* is the perfect time to whistle an old-timey tune. He quiets immediately, and I add, making my way up the back steps of the main Preston house, "Just be very, very quiet."

I unlock the back door and let my friends in first. Logan immediately walks into a chair, and it scrapes along the hardwood floors. Dylan slaps him upside the head while I curse him out. "Do not wake the beast!" I hiss through clenched teeth.

After going through the contents of our pantry and realizing we had fuck all ingredients to actually make a wedding cake, I came up with the brilliant idea of raiding my father-in-law's kitchen. Since Demander had given me and Dylan (who knows why) the task, I could trust that he'd be stealth. Military training, you know? But then Logan overheard, and he was all, "I wanna come! I wanna come!" and so here we are.

It's past midnight.

The house is quiet, all lights off, and I use my phone for a source of light. Dylan, aka Grandpa Banks, doesn't carry a phone when he's with Riley, but he has a mini flashlight attached to his keychain, so that's what he's using. "What are we even looking for?" Dylan asks.

I pull up the basic cake recipe on my phone at the same time Logan opens the fridge and announces, way too loud for my comfort, "Let there be light!"

"Shut the fuck up!" I hiss.

Logan chuckles.

Then the kitchen door opens, and I freeze at the sight in front of me. Sir Tom Preston's gigantic robe-covered frame takes up the entire space of the doorway. That, alone, is intimidating enough, even without the shotgun he has aimed directly at me.

"Want me to disarm him?" Dylan asks, all cool and calm, as if there isn't a man holding a gun right in front of him.

"No," I say at the same time Tom lowers his weapon and flicks on the light.

Tom shakes his head as he says, "What the fuck, son?"

I take stock of the situation and what he must be thinking. Hearing noises downstairs, then opening the door to a dark room only to find three fully grown, yet completely immature, man-children, one of which he let his only daughter marry.

Good times.

Of the three of us, Dylan is the most normal in appearance. I'm still covered in red and yellow ketchup and mustard, courtesy of Jake, and Logan has fragments of eggshells on his forehead. Plus, he's now helping himself to a plate of leftovers he must've found in the fridge.

Class act, we are.

"It's, uh..." My voice wobbles, and I attempt to clear it.

Almost fifteen years of being part of this family and Tom Preston still has the power to unnerve me. Don't get me wrong. I love the man, but that doesn't mean I'm less afraid of him. "It's a long story, sir."

"Not really," Dylan tells him. "Jake and Mikayla decided to have an impromptu wedding, and Amanda tasked us with making a cake."

"A wedding?" Tom asks.

"Yes, sir," Dylan replies.

"Right now?" Tom again.

"Yes, sir."

"And you three are making the cake?"

Logan tells him, "Demander demanded the demands."

"Demander?"

"Amanda the Demander, sir," I retort.

"Dad?" a voice calls from behind Tom. "What's going on?"

Another voice. "Yeah, what's going on?"

Tom moves to the side, revealing the twins, Lincoln and Liam, approaching.

Logan burps. "I think I may have drunk too much. My vision's blurred, and I'm seeing double."

"Ha-ha," Lincoln deadpans. "We've *literally* never heard that one before."

"Literally never," Liam echoes, then asks, "What are you guys doing?"

Tom side-eyes them, answering for us, "Apparently they need ingredients to make a wedding cake."

"Huh," the twins respond, in sync.

Logan sighs. "Now I'm *hearing* double."

I say, trying to defuse the situation, "We'll be out of your hair in, like, two minutes."

Logan lifts the plate he's helped himself to. "This is really good, Mr. Preston. Did you—"

"Yo, that's mine," Lachlan, the youngest Preston at fourteen, appears out of nowhere and steps into the room, taking the plate from Logan and reapplying the cling wrap. He sets it back in the fridge, closes the door, and stands in front of it, arms crossed.

Logan looks from Lachlan to the twins and back again. "Did I just time travel?"

I chuckle. I can't help it. Then I quote a line from my favorite movie. "Where we're going..." I wait for someone to finish it for me, but all I get is dead stares. I mumble to myself, "1.21 gigawatts."

"There should be stuff in the pantry," Tom says after a beat. "I'm going back to bed."

Liam sighs, then quickly moves around the room, grabbing a bunch of ingredients for me. Just between me and me, I've always liked Liam the best, even going back to the days when I coached him in little league. Of all the Preston Punks, Liam gives me the least amount of shit. He hands me flour, some cans of fruit, milk, eggs, sugar and whipped cream. "This should do you."

I open the carton of eggs, collect one, and crack it over Logan's head. Then hand the carton back to him. "We have plenty of these. Thanks, Uncle Twinny," I tell him, using Katie's name for the twins. She can't tell them apart yet, and I understand completely. Based on appearance alone, I only started to tell them apart last year.

"You don't talk much, do you?" Lachlan asks, looking up at Dylan.

Dylan squares his shoulders, crosses his arms, and *grunts*.

Lachlan nods once, then glances my direction. "Cool dude."

"We better get started on this," I tell them, lifting the ingredients. "We're working against the clock."

The Preston boys file out of the kitchen without saying a word, switching off the light as they leave.

I hand Dylan our supplies so I can lock up and then get

back on the golf cart. It's not until we're back at the cabin and have the ingredients set out on the counter that I realize we didn't even get everything the recipe needed. "Shit."

Dylan shoves me out of the way, then rolls up his sleeves. "Don't worry," he says. "I got this."

"You burned the cookies," Logan reminds him.

Dylan chuckles, turning to Logan. "You're not even supposed to be on our team."

"Yeah," I joke. Then mock, "You don't even go here."

"Fuck y'all," Logan laughs out, retrieving a mixing bowl. "Best cake wins. Winner takes all."

"Define *all*," Dylan questions.

Logan pulls out his wallet, slams it on the counter. "Whatever is in there."

I check the wallet, count out the cash. "Two dollars and fifteen cents."

Dylan shakes Logan's hand. "Deal."

GUEST LIST

JAKE
MLB PRO

MIKAYLA
MLB WAG

LOGAN
RESIDENT DOCTOR

AMANDA
CHILD PSYCHOLOGIST

CAMERON
ARCHITECT

LUCY
BOOKSTORE OWNER

DYLAN
MAYHEM MOTORS

RILEY
DYLAN'S BOSS

SPECIAL APPEARANCE

HEIDI
RETAIL BUYER

14

Heidi

Lucy doesn't have a mirrored dresser in her room, so Mikayla and I brought in a chair from the kitchen and set up in the bathroom. I'm not really sure what Amanda meant by "make her look like a bride", but I was too afraid to ask.

I looked for something white in Lucy's closet for Mikayla to wear, but Lucy lives in dark colors, and she's also pint-sized compared to the rest of us, so there's no way anything would fit. And I don't exactly drive around with my makeup collection in the trunk, so I can't do much with Micky's face, not that she needs it. And also, we have completely different skin tones. The most I can offer is to do something with her hair, and so that's where I start.

I watch Mikayla through the mirror as the flat iron preheats and smile when she does. "You're getting married," I say, almost as excited as she is.

"Crazy, right?"

"Are you kidding?" I laugh out. "We've been waiting for this moment forever."

"I know..."

"You don't have to go into detail," I state. "But whatever was holding you back, you've worked it out now?"

Before she has time to respond, there's a knock on the door.

"If you're anyone but Jake, you can enter!"

The door opens, and Roman pops his head in. "Demander said I need to help you. Though, I..." He glances at Mikayla, then me. "I don't really know how much help I'll be."

I don't look at him when I say, "I tried to find something white, *anything*, but I couldn't. Maybe you can try?"

"On it," he replies, closing the door between us.

I settle my hand on Micky's head, ready to get to work, but she shifts, turning to me, her eyes wide. "What?" I ask.

"You're blushing!"

"Shut up! Am not." Maybe a little, but it's hard not to. Roman is *hot*—all dark hair and dark eyes and tanned, masculine arms. Even beneath his sweatshirt, I can tell he's built—

"Heidi!"

"*What*?" I laugh. "So, he's hot? So are a million other guys. I literally just met him tonight. I know nothing about him."

"Jake said he played baseball with him. Didn't you guys go to the same school?"

"Yes, but I don't remember him."

"Ooh," Micky sings, facing the mirror again. "I bet you'll remember him now."

I roll my eyes. "Yeah, and I bet he'll forget me tomorrow."

Mikayla's nose scrunches. "Did he remember you from school?"

"Yeah."

"See?" She raises her eyebrows. "You're impossible to forget."

Shaking my head, I tell her, "Either way, it's not like—" I shut my mouth the second the door opens again. Roman walks in with sheer curtains, toilet paper, and a length of rubber hose.

"Those curtains are from Katie's bed, are they?" Micky asks him.

Roman smiles. "No, but that's where I got the idea. I took these from the curtain rods in the living room. There's more in Cam and Lucy's room if we need them."

"And the toilet paper?" I ask.

He shrugs. "If the curtains weren't appealing."

I giggle, take the fabric from him. "I think this will work."

"And the hose?" Micky asks him.

He looks so proud as he twists the hose to form a ring. "I figure we can join the ends and turn it into a crown or veil somehow."

I gasp. "You are a genius, my friend."

"Thanks." He stands taller. "Sucks they'll need to replace their hose, but whatever, right?" He squeezes Micky's shoulder, adding, "You only get married once." And then he turns to the door again. "I'm going to find some tape."

"So resourceful," Micky says once he's left. "Good boyfriend qualities."

"Quit it." I aim the flat iron at her head. "Loose curls?"

She nods. "Loose curls."

When Roman returns a few minutes later, he has another set of curtains, scissors and tape. "I have an idea," he announces, all giddy with excitement. "You mind if I make the veil?"

"Go ahead," I answer. "I'm not your boss."

"Not yet," Micky murmurs.

I shove her shoulder, causing her to laugh. "Ignore her," I tell Roman, who's looking so adorably confused. He sets himself up *in* the bathtub with all his supplies and gets right to work.

For a solid minute, no one speaks as I work on Micky's hair, and Roman cuts strips out of the curtain. Not that I'm watching him. In fact, I'm trying my hardest to ignore his very presence. Me and boys right now? Not a good mix.

Micky breaks the silence. "I bet you have the most amazing, elaborate wedding planned."

Internally, I lock up. Externally, I say, "Me?"

"No, *Roman*."

Roman looks up from his task, pulling out an earphone I didn't know was there. "Huh?"

"Nothing," Micky laughs. "Please resume listening to whatever you're listening to." She waits while Roman nods slowly, replaces the earphone, and gets back to work. Then continues, "I bet you have it all planned out. Where it is, what you're wearing... oh, I bet it's a destination wedding!"

I lower my gaze, focus on the curls I'm providing. "I don't think so," I tell her honestly. "I think I've come to terms with the fact that I'm never going to walk down the aisle."

"Heidi," she scoffs. "It's not like you have an expiration date. We're still young!"

"No, I know," I rush out. "It's not the age thing. I just... I haven't felt anything substantial with anyone for a while." I glance over at Roman, but he's so focused on his task, I don't think he's even paying attention. "There was Dylan, but that was a first love kind of thing. There was no one after him in college, and then I came back here, and all the good boys were gone, so..."

"So you moved to Atlanta to find love?"

"Not *just* for that." I needed a fresh start somewhere else. Somewhere where I wasn't Heidi from high school or Dylan's ex, and to be honest, I felt like I needed a new set of friends. Not to *replace* these ones, but just... so I didn't feel so much like an outsider all the time. I realized, far too quickly, that the things you may have in common with people don't make for a solid foundation for friendship. I was twenty-three when I moved to Atlanta. I'm twenty-nine now, and I spent all those years searching for something else. Something *more*. With friends, with relationships, with a job or career I could get excited about. I never found it.

"Why Atlanta?" Micky asks, pulling me from my thoughts.

When I moved, I told everyone it was for a job prospect. There was no job. There was just... opportunity, I guess. This time, I tell Micky the truth. "You know the sports bar on Main?"

"Yeah."

"They have this map of the U.S. on the wall, and one night, I was there with Cam and Luce, and we were playing darts, and... I aimed at the map and *boom*, Atlanta."

Micky laughs, and I do, too. It's kind of crazy, when I think about it, but it felt right at the time.

"What happened to that one guy you dated for, like, two years?" she asks. "Surely there was something substantial there? Some sparks, at least?"

"Oh, there were sparks all right. But sparks fade. And his faded first."

"I'm sorry," she says. "Did it make you scared to try again?"

"I don't know..." I think about it for a moment, my gaze lost in my task. "I don't really know what I want, you know? And I think, by this point, I should've figured it out. I have no prospects, no career."

"Yeah, I get that," Micky murmurs.

She has Jake—a man she's literally about to marry. I keep that thought to myself, and I'm glad I do, because she elaborates.

"I was just telling Jake how I kind of felt the same way... that everything I have is because of him. It's not the best feeling in the world to realize that while I'm extremely grateful and blessed to have him, it doesn't deter from the fact that I feel like I've achieved nothing on my own."

I ponder her words for a long moment, and as sad as it is that she feels that way, she's also right. Not in a *bad* way. It's just the way their lives played out. I never thought about it from her perspective before, because I always just saw it as her supporting him, which no doubt takes work, but I can totally understand how she feels.

"We should go into business together," she says, and I can't tell if she's joking or not.

"Yeah, that would be amazing." Even the mere mention of it has me more excited than going back to my empty apartment in Atlanta and my crappy job as a social media manager and buyer for a crappy retail clothing chain. "But doing what?"

"I don't know," she laughs out. "I'm sure we could think of something."

Maybe.

Maybe not.

"All done," I state, clicking the flat iron twice before unplugging it from the wall. I turn to Roman, who's been silent the entire time. "How you doing with that veil?" I ask.

He doesn't respond, too busy working away.

I reach over, tap his shoulder. He looks up, dark brown eyes right on mine. "I'm almost done!" he shouts over the music only he can hear. "Don't look! It's a surprise!"

I hold my hands up in mock surrender. "Okay..."

Mikayla giggles, and I settle my hands on her shoulders. "Maybe we should give you just a tiny bit of color on your lips," I suggest.

"I think Lucy has some stuff in the drawers."

I open the first draw, nothing. Then the second. I immediately close it. "How many fucking sex toys do those two have?"

"Done!" Roman announces, hopping out of the bathtub and handing his work over to me.

"Roman!" Micky gasps.

"Holy shit!" I echo her sentiment, staring down at the masterpiece in awe. He's braided strips of the curtain and twisted it around the hose, so you can't even tell what it once was. And in the strands of the braid, he's tied long ribbons of fabric to make the "train" and one long solid piece to go over the face. "Roman, this is..."

He grins so wide, so proud, it makes me feel the same. "It's good, huh?"

"It's *beautiful*."

"How do you know how to braid?" Micky asks him.

He shrugs. "I have a little sister. Well, she's not so little anymore, but she was once, obviously..."

"And you braided her hair?" I coo.

He side-eyes the both of us, completely confused by our response. "Yeah?"

Micky and I share a glance, pouting and sharing an, "Awww."

"That's so adorable," Micky adds, then makes sure to get my attention when she adds, "Good dad qualities."

I stifle my giggle while Roman looks even more confused.

"Stand up. Time to work on the dress."

Roman lies back in the bathtub and closes the shower curtain, as if Micky's about to strip. She's not. I do my best with what I have, which isn't much. It's too cold out to reveal any skin, so I just lay the fabric over her clothes and use safety pins to pin it in place, creating shape where I can. It takes *way* longer than I thought, and when I'm done, I say, "It's not the best, but it'll have to do."

"I'm sure it's perfect," Micky says.

I say over my shoulder. "What do you think, Roman?"

There's no response, and so I turn to the tub, slide open the curtain, ready to get his attention. But... I'm pretty sure the man is *asleep*. Sitting upright, his hands linked and on his lap, his chest rises and falls in a slow rhythm.

I turn to Micky, who grimaces, and then, as quietly as possible, I flick on the shower, busting out a laugh when Roman gasps the second the spray of water hits him. "What the—" He's quick to come to. Quick to realize who's responsible for his soaking, and I'm slow... way too slow to react when his hands reach out for me, lifting me over the lip of the bath and directly on top of him. I scream, wiggling as I try to get out of his hold and avoid the oncoming spray.

Micky laughs, then shouts over the chaos, "I'll be right back!"

I manage to flip over and turn off the stream, just as the front door opens and Amanda calls out, "Ready when you are! I'll leave a flashlight by the door!"

Cool.

Great.

Awesome.

Roman has an erection, and I know, because I'm straddling it.

I clear my throat, avoid all eye contact, and quickly hop out of the bath.

Roman does the same, minus the throat clearing. He does, however, adjust himself, right at my eye level as I attempt to towel off any excess water from my jeans.

"I'm hard, and you're so damn wet," he says out of nowhere, his voice low, *rough.*

Eyes wide in shock, I pop my head up and screech, *"What?"*

After a chuckle, he grabs another towel and starts drying his hair. "It's so easy to mess with you."

I shake my head, trying to ignore the inferno he just lit deep inside me. Too bad that heat won't do anything for me outside. "I'm going to freeze out on that dock."

"Nah, I'll keep you warm."

Standing to full height, I lift my chin and lock my eyes on his. I can't tell if he's still messing with me or... "Are you flirting with me, Roman..." *Shit.* "What's your last name?"

He smirks—a wicked little sight that has my pulse racing. "You'll have to go flipping through some old yearbooks for that one."

"Hmm." It's all I say before I open the door to make my escape. A sea of bodies greets me, all large and masculine and turned away from me. Logan, Dylan and Cam are standing just outside the closed bedroom door, and they all turn to me when I ask, "What's going on?"

Cam speaks for all of them, his voice just above a whisper. "We weren't sure if she wanted one of us to walk her down the aisle or..."

My shoulders drop as I eye each of them one by one and, suddenly, it occurs to me *why* I've had so much trouble with the men in my life. It's because I hold them to the same standard as the three men standing in front of me. I met them as boys—all impulse and bravado, and maybe a little immaturity, but they were always respectful. Always considerate. Always loyal—to their girls and to each other. Through the years, they've only grown in those sentiments. And my love for them, as brothers, has grown with it.

I push down the knot in my throat, the ache in my chest. "Did you ask her?"

"Not yet," Dylan answers.

Logan adds, "We don't really know how to bring it up..."

I push between them and knock gently on the door. "Micky, the guys are out here... Did you want one of them to walk you down—"

"No!" she interrupts. "You guys go ahead. I just need a few minutes."

GUEST LIST

JAKE
MLB PRO

MIKAYLA
MLB WAG

LOGAN
RESIDENT DOCTOR

AMANDA
CHILD PSYCHOLOGIST

CAMERON
ARCHITECT

LUCY
BOOKSTORE OWNER

DYLAN
MAYHEM MOTORS

RILEY
DYLAN'S BOSS

SPECIAL APPEARANCE

HEIDI
RETAIL BUYER

15

Jake

Girls are made of magic, and I say this as a man who has absolutely no idea how they managed to pull off what they have in the short time that was given to them.

The end of the dock is lined with tiki torches, giving us the heat we need to be out here. There are string lights hung between the posts of the dock, and candles and lanterns every few feet, from one end to the other, paving the way to the makeshift altar. The "flower arrangements" are nothing more than cut off pieces of Lucy and Cam's Christmas tree placed into glass jars, and there are eight chairs in total, four on one side, four on the other—just enough for our friends who are here. One chair will be empty, because Logan's standing right next to me, ready to officiate.

Everything looks amazing, and I feel...

I feel great, I guess, except that I'm in a suit two sizes too small, and I'm freezing, and...

And I've been standing here for ten minutes, looking out at the end of the dock, waiting for my "bride-to-be."

Every few seconds, one of my friends turns around, looking for her, too.

No one says a word, but I know what they're thinking, because I'm thinking it, too. *She's changed her mind.*

Maybe I went about it the wrong way. Maybe I didn't *hear* what she was trying to tell me. Sure, I listened, but maybe I should've—

One of the girls gasps, and I lift my eyes toward the end of the dock. I can make out an outline of a body, but that's basically it. I stand taller, my nerves suddenly shot. But then another body appears, and then another, and behind me, Logan says, out loud, what I'm thinking. "What the fuck?"

The people approach, and once they're close enough to make out their appearance, my shoulders drop again. "Mom?"

She waits until she's right in front of me, her eyes scanning me from head to toe. "Kayla called and told us to come down here... directly to the dock. She said something good and *big* was happening." She looks around, at the lights and the candles and the fake trees in makeshift vases, and then back at me. Then she runs a hand over my suit while my dad and sister, Julie, stop behind her. "What's going on?" she asks, even though I can see in her eyes that she already knows the answer to her question.

I smile. It feels forced, though I know it shouldn't be. This is, after all, exactly what *I* wanted. "I'm getting married, Ma."

The pain in her eyes has me looking away. "Oh."

"I know," I mumble. "I'm sorry." It's not as if my mom is one of those types who needs to be involved in every aspect of my life, but... I'm her only son, and this is my only wedding. She helped me pick out the engagement ring and cried when I bought it, because she knew how much Kayla would love it.

I don't know.

I guess giving her a little heads-up would've been nice.

"This is what you want?" she asks, and I force myself to look at her.

She's on the verge of tears, and I can't decipher the reasoning.

I push past the pain in my chest and take her hand in mine, squeezing once. "Yes, I want to *marry* her." It's all I've wanted for so long.

"Then that's all that matters," Dad says, speaking for the first time since they got here. "We want what you want, and we're happy for you, son."

He offers me his hand, and I shake it. "Thanks, Dad." Then I hug my mom, followed by my sister.

My friends have already moved seats, leaving the front row for my family while the guys stand at the back. As soon as my family is seated, music plays through speakers somewhere around us, and I look up just in time to see Kayla step onto the dock. She's in the same clothes she was in before, but now she's covered in sheer white fabric, and she's holding a bouquet of plastic branches. The veil covers her face, so I can't see her clearly, but I already know she's beautiful.

She always is.

I suck in a breath, my shoulders rising with the action, and wait the few seconds it takes for her to get to me.

"Hi," I say.

"Hi," she responds.

I lift the veil, revealing her eyes—eyes that turn amber beneath the flames of the tiki torch.

"You look beautiful."

Her laugh is soft. Her smile softer. Then she looks over at my family. "Sorry to wake you," she tells them. "And thank you for coming."

"Of course, sweetheart," Mom says, her voice shaking with emotion as she wipes the tears off her cheeks. "Thank you for inviting us."

Logan clears his throat, then asks, "Are we ready?"

"Yeah." I reach for Kayla's hands, but they're too busy holding the branches. Mom's quick to take them from her, then retake her seat.

"Short and sweet, right?" Logan whispers, confirming my earlier request.

"Short and sweet," I tell him.

"Okay. You got the rings?"

My eyes snap to his. "The *rings*." I stupidly pat my pockets, as if two rings will somehow appear out of thin air.

"I got you," Dad says, struggling to remove his wedding ring, then doing the same with my mom's. I don't think I've ever seen them without their rings the entire time I've been alive. Not once. He gets up to give Kayla his and gives Mom's to me and then quickly sits back down. "Go ahead."

I look at the ring between my fingers, at the inscription inside with their initials and wedding date. There are pictures of their wedding around the house, of them cutting the cake and sharing their first dance. You could see it in their eyes, how deep their love ran, how excited they were to declare the rest of their lives as one.

"Jake," Kayla whispers, and I lift my gaze to her tear-soaked eyes.

I *knew* it. Even before my family showed up... even before *she* appeared, I knew something was wrong. "It's okay," I murmur.

She tries hard, *so* hard, to contain her sob, but the moment it's out, she falls into me. I hold her close, repeat, "It's okay." I place my mouth to her ear, whisper the words, "We don't have to do this. I didn't mean to pressure you—"

"No." She pulls away, neck craned to look up at me. "That's not it."

"Then what is it?"

"Just keep holding me a minute," she asks, and so I do. I'd

hold her for a minute. A lifetime. It doesn't matter. And I'll wait for her. We all will. Because we know when she's ready, she'll give us everything she has, everything she is. Every perfect piece of her. Eventually, she pulls back slightly, kissing me once before saying, loud enough for everyone to hear, "As soon as the courthouse opens and we can legally marry, we'll do it. I want nothing more in this world than to be your wife and for you to be my husband, and I don't want you to have to go another day questioning that. Heck, you may as well start calling me your wife, because there's no stopping it now."

I laugh once, relief pouring through me in waves. "That sounds like a solid plan." And then I kiss her, the way I've wanted to since I saw her walking toward me. "Wait," I say, backing up slightly. "Does that mean we're not doing this?"

Kayla presses her lips tight, sucking in air through her nose, as she turns to the people closest to us. "Thank you guys so much," she says, motioning to our surroundings. "Thank you for putting all of this together on such short notice." She focuses on my family. "Thank you for coming when I called, and not asking questions... It's just..." Kayla looks up at me, tears welling in her eyes.

I nod, offer an encouraging smile. I understand why it took her years to open up to me, just like I understand why it was so hard to do so. More than anything, though, I held on to the faith that when she was ready, she would. And I know... I feel it in my gut... she's ready now.

She faces the world head on, her shoulders back, chin raised. "You know, I was dreading coming here tonight. Not to see you all, but coming *here*, to the cabin. The thing is, I've been thinking about my family a lot lately. More about their deaths than their lives... and this place... it's the last time I was truly happy while they were still alive. I left here that night thinking I had the world at my feet, and then... it was all ripped away from me, but now? Now, I think it's time to replace those memories with new ones. With *good* ones." Kayla chokes on a sob but finds the strength to continue. "I... I said no to Jake in the past, because I couldn't imagine a wedding without my family, but as I stand here, I realize that I *have* a family... in all of you. So... if it's okay with your family, Luce, I'd really like to come back here, on the anniversary of their deaths, and have a proper wedding. A *celebration*."

"Of course!" Lucy cries, wiping her tears.

Kayla takes my mom's ring from me and approaches my parents. "And, Nathan," she says to my dad, handing him back his ring. "I'd really love it if the man who's been my father-figure for over a decade would consider walking me down the aisle?"

"Aw, honey." I've never seen my dad cry. I see it now. "I would be honored."

Kayla hugs him tight, and I picture a much younger version of her doing the same with her father, looking up at the strong-est, bravest man in her world. Then she turns to my mom, giving her ring back, and then my sister. "Would you mind helping me plan and maybe taking me dress shopping?"

My mom and sister are too emotional to speak, so they just hug her, the way my dad did.

Tears blur my vision, and I look around at our friends, at all the girls crying and the guys comforting them. Behind me, Logan sniffs, and I turn to him just as he wipes at his eyes. "It's the wind. Shut up."

I chuckle under my breath, wiping at my own eyes, then taunt him with a whispered, "You're such a little bitch."

He glares at me, then whispers back, "So is *your mom*."

"I heard that, Logan," Mom sings.

Logan drops his head between his shoulders. "Sorry, ma'am."

"Little bitch," I tease.

"Knock it off, Jacob," Dad orders, and I cower under his words, then giggle like an idiot with my best friend.

Logan steps around me and says, in true Logan fashion, "Listen, this is cool and all, happy for your future wedding, blah blah blah, but I made a cake from scratch!"

"Jesus, Logan!" Amanda admonishes at the same time Cam and Dylan say in unison, "So did we!"

Then Amanda yells at Logan, "You weren't even *on* cake duty!"

Kayla laughs at their antics. "We can still have your cakes!"

Logan stomps his foot. "Not if there isn't a damn wedding!"

"Wait!" Roman yells, and all eyes go to him.

GUEST LIST

JAKE MIKAYLA
MLB PRO · MLB WAG

LOGAN ♥ AMANDA
RESIDENT DOCTOR · CHILD PSYCHOLOGIST

CAMERON ♥ LUCY
ARCHITECT · BOOKSTORE OWNER

DYLAN ♥ RILEY
MAYHEM MOTORS · DYLAN'S BOSS

SPECIAL APPEARANCE

HEIDI
RETAIL BUYER

16

Heidi

Roman is looking at me.

Why is Roman looking at me?

Why is he smirking at me?

Why is he leaning in close to me?

Is he about to kiss me?

Absolutely not.

"You said you thought you'd never walk down the aisle," he says, and my eyes widen in shock. "There's an aisle right here."

I'm fully aware that everyone is watching me, watching *us*, and so I roll my eyes, try to play it cool. "I mean down the aisle... toward the man of my dreams."

He pulls back, straightening his spine, then points a thumb at himself, that smirk never leaving him. "I'm right here."

This is insane. Ridiculous. *Outlandish.*

"Wedding," someone whispers, and that whisper turns into a chant. "Wedding! Wedding!" Until everyone's saying it, stomping their feet in between bursts of laughter. "Wedding! Wedding! Wedding! Wedd—"

"Fine," I yell and immediately wish I could take it back.

The cheers that follow have me shaking my head.

"We'll get out of your hair," Jake's dad says.

"We'll walk you to your car," Jake replies.

Micky turns to me, eyes narrowed, finger stabbing through the air. "Don't you dare start without us."

"Veil," I ask, palm up between us.

Micky smiles, removing the veil and handing it to me. "It was *always* yours."

I have no idea what that means, but I plop the veil on my head anyway.

"Hot," Roman declares, shoving his hands in his pockets as he rocks on his heels.

My head tilts to the side as I try to get a read on him. "Is this your thing?" I ask. "Meet a girl, marry her?"

He chuckles, but doesn't respond.

"I bet you're a one and done kind of guy, huh? Mister One-Night Stand?"

He pushes forward, leans in *real* close. "It's the tattoos, isn't it?"

I bite back a burst of laughter, then look over at my friends. They're all huddled around the two cakes while Logan, Cam and Dylan argue about which one looks the best. I turn to Roman, grab his arm, and roll up his sleeve, inspecting the aforementioned tattoos. It's too dark to see them intricately, but I can make out a cross, a bird, and a ribbon flowing through them. "Where'd you get them done? Prison?" I joke.

"No, but I met the guy who does them there," he deadpans.

I look up, expecting the same smirk from earlier. It's no longer there. "I can't tell if you're joking."

He shakes his head. "No jokes."

I focus on his arm again, twist it to get a better look. There's an unopened envelope with the initials AB on the corner. I'm not even going to question who AB is. Instead, I ask, "What were you in prison for?"

"The usual," he replies, all nonchalant.

I've met people who have been in prison before, but I never really cared enough to know why, or how, they got there. I care about Roman, though, and I don't know what that means yet. "Elaborate?"

"Possession with intent to sell."

Hmm. "Are you still involved with that?"

"I wouldn't be working two jobs, six days a week, if I was."

"Valid point." I trace the ribbon with a single finger. "Did you do it for kicks or out of necessity?"

"The latter."

I glance up at him. He watches me back. "So, you met your tattoo artist in prison?"

"Yep." He takes his arm back, pulling the sleeve back down. "He was my cellmate. He's this forty-five-year-old short, stocky Filipino dude named Juan. Amazing artist, but didn't know what to do with his talent, so I told him he should look into tattooing. He got out before me, but when I was released, he was out in the parking lot waiting for me."

I didn't ask for all this information, but I like the fact that he's willing to supply it. And I like it even more that he doesn't hide who he is or *was*.

"He brought me back to his house, introduced me to his wife and kids, and showed me the tattoo gear he'd bought. He hadn't used it yet, so I let him practice on me. I don't even know half the shit that's on my body."

I'm smiling, and I don't really know why. "I like Juan," I tell him.

He laughs at that. "Everyone likes Juan. It's kind of impossible not to."

"So, I take it you still keep in touch."

"Yeah," he says, nodding. "I spent the day with him and his

family and half the neighborhood." He motions behind me, to Jake and Micky walking up the dock, hand in hand. "You ready to be Mrs. Baker?"

I grin up at him. "You just saved me from flipping through my old yearbooks, Roman Baker."

He rolls his eyes, then blesses me with that smirk again. "Let's do the damn thing."

"What song do you want?" Amanda asks.

I freeze a moment, thinking, and giggle to myself as I make my way over to her and whisper my song choice in her ear.

Her grin matches mine. "You got it."

After walking the length of the dock, I turn and face the altar, then wait. Once the first few chords of "What Makes You Beautiful" by One Direction start, I don't just *walk* down the aisle. I fucking *strut,* stopping to dance and sing, aka *scream*, the lyrics with my girls. It is, by far, the most joy I've felt in the longest time, and I realize now, a little too late, that regardless of the physical distance—or the emotional one I've created between us—these people are *still* my friends for a reason.

I came here tonight because I didn't want to be home alone on Christmas.

But that house, the home I grew up in—it isn't my home.

The people here are.

When the song finishes, I walk toward Roman, who's watched me the entire time with a giant grin on his face. When I get close enough, he offers me his hands, and for a long moment, we just stand there, holding hands and looking into each other's eyes, our smiles growing with each passing second.

And, because Logan is Logan and his main priority is finding out who won the best cake contest, his officiant speech goes a little like this:

Logan: "Roman, say I do."

Roman: "I do."

Logan: "Heids, same shit."

Me: "I do."

Logan: "Now kiss."

Full disclosure: I didn't think about the whole kissing thing when I agreed to this, but the moment Roman steps toward me, I freeze. And when his hand cradles my neck, his thumb under my chin, lifting my face up to his, I stop breathing. And when his mouth meets mine, I...

I black out.

Maybe.

Just a little bit.

I know that his touch is warm, and that his lips are soft, and that his tongue tastes like mint...

But... I don't know how long we kissed for, and I don't know what he sees when he pulls away and finally opens his eyes.

What I do know is that happened just now, I want it to happen again.

And again.

And again.

"Welp," Lucy announces. "I got a stiff clitty!"

Me, too, Luce.

Me. Fucking. Too.

GUEST LIST

JAKE
MLB PRO

MIKAYLA
MLB WAG

LOGAN
RESIDENT DOCTOR

AMANDA
CHILD PSYCHOLOGIST

CAMERON
ARCHITECT

LUCY
BOOKSTORE OWNER

DYLAN
MAYHEM MOTORS

RILEY
DYLAN'S BOSS

SPECIAL APPEARANCE

HEIDI
RETAIL BUYER

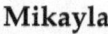

17

Mikayla

Both impromptu wedding cakes are horrid, and not a single one of us was prepared for just how bad they would be. Not even the guys who made them.

They're both now in the lake, and we're still at the dock while Logan stares me down, trying to communicate with his eyes alone.

Since it was supposed to be *my* wedding, the boys had already decided that I would be the judge of their little contest, which, the rest of us are just finding out now, has a grand prize of two dollars and fifteen cents.

"Logan wins," I blurt out, just to get it over with.

"Victory!" Logan yells, arms in the air.

"Are you fucking kidding me?" Cameron groans, looking over at Dylan, who is... fast asleep, sitting upright in a chair.

Cam busts out a guffaw, and Logan coos, "Aww, poor Grandpa Banks. It's way past his bedtime."

"He was awake, like, a minute ago," Jake chimes in.

"Yeah, this is completely normal for him," Riley says through a yawn. "I think it's time to call it a night."

Logan steps up to her, his hands up in a prayer position. "*Please* let me push his ass into the lake."

"No!" Riley laughs, passing him to get to her husband. She shakes him awake, saying, "Let's get you home, Grandpa."

Dylan grumbles, like a true old man, and comes to a stand.

"You owe me two dollars and fifteen cents," Logan reminds him.

"Yeah?" Dylan grunts. "Take it out of the money *your mom* owes me."

Logan pouts, exaggerates a sob. "I don't have a mom, you asshole."

For a second, Dylan almost looks sorry for his slip. But before he can apologize, Logan *attempts* to push him into the lake. Dylan is the biggest of all the boys, so Logan's efforts are futile, but it sparks a comical rage in Dylan, and the next thing you know, Dylan's chasing him down the dock, and the other boys follow, cursing each other while laughing hysterically.

The girls and I take our time, lagging behind them.

"You'll let us know if you need any help with the wedding planning, right?" Amanda asks.

"Of course."

"And don't pay for anyone to move or carry anything," Lucy says. "That's what all my brothers are for."

"I don't want to exploit them," I laugh out. "And thank you for letting me have it here."

"Please, we're honored to host it."

I look past Amanda next to me and toward Heidi. "You'll fly home for it, right?"

"Girl, I wouldn't miss it for the world."

"How long are you in town for?" Riley asks her.

"I haven't booked a flight home yet, so..." she trails off.

Lucy says, "You should all come over in a couple of days once we're settled into the new house. And you can give your presents to Katie in person. She would love that."

"*I* would love that," Heidi says. "I was sad I didn't get to see her."

"You know you're welcome to come over whenever."

"Yeah?" Heidi asks.

"Heidi!" Lucy snaps. "You're always welcome. You never need an invitation."

"Okay." Heidi smiles over at her. "I'll keep that in mind."

Lucy says, "It's decided. Two days from now. Our new house. We'll order takeout. Everyone come." Her next words are for Heidi. "And I'll make sure to invite Rooooman."

"Holy shit, that was some kiss," Amanda cracks.

"You're telling me," Heidi mumbles.

"So, you felt it, huh?" I ask. "Something *substantial?*"

"Maybe," Heidi admits. "Or maybe it was just sparks... and you know what happens with sparks? They fade."

Before any of us can retort, Dylan yelling has us all freezing momentarily.

"Oh, no," Riley sighs. "What did they do?"

Beside me, Lucy giggles. "Let's just say the King of Mayhem has met his match."

We hasten our steps, giggling at the curses being thrown around and the boys' guffaws that accompany it. By the time we make it to the front of the cabin, Dylan is... Dylan.

Silent.

Deadly.

We all wait for the next move.

The next sound.

It doesn't come from him, though.

It comes from Riley.

She busts out a laugh so loud and free that it makes us all

do the same. "Babe!" She's laughing so hard; tears form in her eyes. "You thought you were safe!" Her hand goes to her stomach. "How did this even happen?"

"Six brothers," Cam informs, pointing to Lucy.

I move closer to Dylan's truck to get a better look.

Since he opened his shop, he's had a white decal on the side with his phone number and the company logo—Mayhem Motors and an image of tire marks behind the text. That decal is gone now, replaced with a bright pink one, similar design, only now it says, "Mayhem Male Escorts" with an image of a dildo instead of the tire marks. The phone number is the same. But that's not even the best part. They didn't just replace the one that was originally there. They applied smaller versions of it, at least a hundred of them, all over the truck.

Let me reiterate. These aren't like bumper stickers. They're decals, which means each separate letter has to be removed one by one.

It's pure mayhem genius, and I can't stop laughing. Neither can Jake, who sidles up behind me and wraps his arms around me. "So good," he says.

"*So* good," I agree.

"How the fuck did they have time to do it without me noticing?" Dylan asks.

"We gave them the key to your truck. They drove it away and did it," Cam tells him.

Dylan pats his pocket. "I've had my keys on me the whole time."

"Not the spare key," Roman retorts, smirking. "That one you keep at the shop."

Dylan presses his lips together, nodding slowly. "Well, you're fired."

Roman chuckles.

"No, you're not," Riley assures.

"Babe!" Dylan argues, smacking the bed. "Have you seen the back?"

Riley makes her way to the back of the truck, and whatever she sees only makes her laugh harder. Amanda, Heidi and I join her, cracking up at the sight. Another decal, *huge* letters: *Free Butt Plugs For All.*

"Let's go," Dylan tells Riley, opening the passenger side door. "We need to speed home so no one sees it."

"Relax," Riley tells him. "You've done much worse to them. Or do you forget the time you electrocuted Logan?"

"He still has nightmares about it," Amanda chimes in.

"Or that time you accidentally, yet *actually*, poisoned Jake."

Jake groans.

"That was years ago," Dylan defends.

"Or that time you set fire to Cameron's balls."

Dylan chuckles. "That was a good one."

"Yeah, that was good," Logan agrees.

"Fuck you," Cam snaps at Logan, then glares at Dylan. "Fuck you." He focuses on Jake. "Fuck you because you were there." And then he points to Roman. "And fuck you because you're laughing about it."

Riley tells Dylan, "The only one you haven't messed with is—"

"Roman," Dylan cuts in, rubbing his hands together gleefully. "You better count your days, *buddy.*"

Roman laughs. "I'll mark them off on my calendar, *buddy.*"

Riley starts to get in the car, but stops halfway to ask Heidi, "Are you all right to drive? We can give you a ride home."

"Yeah, that's probably best," Heidi answers.

"I'll give you a ride," Roman tells her, throwing his arm around her shoulders. "It's the least I can do for my *wife.*"

"Speaking of wife," Cam says, looking around. "Where the fuck is mine?"

We all look behind us, where Lucy stands, looking up at the cabin.

"Babe?" Cam asks, walking toward her. We all follow him. "What's wrong?"

"You guys," Lucy says over her shoulder. "This is the last time we'll all be here together like this."

Cam hugs her from behind, and slowly, we form into a line. Us girls in the front, and our men behind us.

"It seemed so much bigger when we were sixteen," Jake muses, his arms around my waist.

For minutes, we all just stare at the cabin, taking it in for everything it is. Memories flash through my mind... not just of the first time I was here, but all the times after. All the book clubs when we talked passionately about fictional characters. The summer days spent out on the lake, followed by summer nights eating pizza and watching *High School Musical* for the umpteenth time. The hours we spent here, as a group, waiting for them to bring home their daughter for the first time.

We've laughed and cried here.

Liked and loathed.

Celebrated and commiserated.

And we've *loved.*

God, have we loved.

Emotion clogs my airways as I recall all the moments we shared here.

The moments when we grew together... and fell apart the same way.

If I feel like this, I can't even imagine how Lucy feels.

"It's so much *more* than a cabin," Heidi murmurs, echoing my thoughts.

"So much *more* than a home," Amanda adds.

"It's where friendships were formed..." Riley says.

"And where first loves were found..." Lucy sighs.

I take Jake's hands, wrap his arms around me tighter. "And where family is forever."

The End

A More Than Mayhem Wedding (A novella), coming mid-2025.

ALSO BY JAY MCLEAN

Sign up to Jay McLean's Newsletter
http://www.jaymcleanauthor.com

Visit Jay McLean's Website
http://www.jaymcleanauthor.com

See all Jay McLean books on Amazon & Kindle Unlimited
https://amzn.to/3RimSvg

See Jay McLean on Goodreads
https://bit.ly/4ccugAp

Jay McLean books on BookBub
https://bit.ly/3kAmshQ

ABOUT THE AUTHOR

 Jay McLean is an international best-selling author and full-time reader, writer of New Adult and Young Adult romance, and skilled procrastinator. When she's not doing any of those things, she can be found running after her three boys, investing way too much time on True Crime Documentaries and binge-watching reality TV.

She writes what she loves to read, which are books that can make her laugh, make her hurt and make her feel.

Jay lives in the suburbs of Melbourne, Australia, in her dream home where music is loud and laughter is louder.

Connect With Jay
www.jaymcleanauthor.com
jay@jaymcleanauthor.com